MURDER

at the
Tokyo American Club

MURDER
at the
Tokyo American Club

Robert J. Collins

YENBOOKS

To Cork
who had the kindred whimsey
to publish this as a newspaper serial before
anyone, including the author,
knew the outcome.

YENBOOKS are published and distributed by
the Charles E. Tuttle Company, Inc. with
editorial offices at 2-6 Suido 1-chome,
Bunkyo-ku, Tokyo 112, Japan

©1991 by Robert J. Collins

First YENBOOKS edition, 1991
Second printing, 1992

LCC Card No. 90-83519
ISBN No. 0-8048-1673-5

Printing in Japan

MURDER
at the
Tokyo American Club

CHAPTER

1

It reminded him suddenly of the half-eaten cockroach in the ham-salad sandwich.

He couldn't have been more than four or five at the time, yet the event was sufficiently impressive to record itself permanently in the section of his brain responsible for cataloging, storing, and reproducing on otherwise slow evenings the fodder for a lifetime of nightmares.

On his best behavior, he sat in his assigned chair at one end of the table in the fancy department-store restaurant. His grandmother chatted merrily with her ladyfriends at the other end. A post luncheon trip to the toy department was the promised reward for "good little boys who are seen but not heard." He was surrounded by quiet civility, the scent of lilacs, and blue hair.

The discovery of cockroach parts gave pause for a moment or two of thoughtful reflection upon the special crispiness of the sandwich as consumed so far. A piece of ham, or lettuce, was stuck in an area of the mouth until recently occupied by a perfectly good baby tooth.

It is altogether conceivable, he mused, that events can seem to be so awful that they can't possibly be real. A lifetime of listening to the tales of the Brothers Grimm had developed in him a healthy skepticism about perceived horrors visiting the good guys. In the stories, the good guys survive all terrors unscathed.

But here was the cockroach, or at least a portion of it, clearly in evidence. He felt an overwhelming urge to communicate directly with his grandmother, seated sedately at the other end of the table. It would appear that awful events *could* be real.

He remembers solving the breaking-into-her-conversation issue rather effectively. In fact, the attention he gained impressively overflowed the circle of his grandmother and her friends and rippled to the very edge of the fancy department-store restaurant. Still in his "best behavior" mode, he screamed at the top of his lungs.

And then for good measure, he threw up.

Now, some forty years later, the "could something so awful be real" question struck again. Standing at the window of the fourth and top floor of the Tokyo American Club, Gordon W. Sparks surveyed the scene below. Rows of neatly parked cars glimmered in the glow of lights surrounding the club's perimeter. On the other side of the parking lot wall stood the Soviet Embassy, a neighbor with whom the American Club shared a relationship fraught with complexity more on paper than in reality. As usual at this time of night, the embassy compound was dark, with only pinpoints of light randomly flashing through branches of the massive trees on the grounds.

Across the club courtyard stood the four-story recreation building, its white walls looking newer and cleaner under artificial illumination than in the harsh light of day. Behind the recreation building and beyond the property, high-rise office and apartment buildings dropped off into the middle distance below the club's hill. Traffic on elevated highways wove as pearls on strings through the masses of concrete that formed the world's largest city. In the far distance lay Tokyo Bay, and then the Pacific beyond.

In the middle of the courtyard was the architectural, and during most months of the year, social centerpiece of the club. The swimming pool and surrounding deck area were an extravagance in open space rarely found in Japan's population centers. On this evening in December, however, the pool area seemed strangely small without the deck chairs, umbrellas, tables, and people.

The underwater lights in the pool had been turned on—an aesthetic concession to club members attending the annual formal dinner-dance. The rippling water cast moving shadows on the recreation building's white wall. Gordon was surprised to notice how vivid the dark lane lines were on the blue bottom of the pool—one rarely saw them through relatively still water.

Without thinking, Gordon loosened his black bow tie and unbuttoned his tuxedo jacket. He started for the ballroom door, then returned to the window for one final check. The ham-salad-sandwich episode flashed into his consciousness. In a daze, he turned and entered the ballroom.

The chandeliers had been dimmed, dishes cleared, and the band members were positioning themselves on the stage. Elegant couples sat at tables decorated with red candles and holly, or sauntered through the groupings of tables to the dance floor. Gordon's table, and his wife, were on the far side of the room.

"Wait a minute!" he yelled to the bandleader, who was just turning away from the audience. The sound was lost to all but those in his immediate vicinity. "Wait a minute!" he bellowed again, still not attracting much attention. The bandleader was raising his arms to signal the downbeat when Gordon W. Sparks did what sort of came naturally. He screamed at the top of his lungs.

And to punctuate his announcement, he threw up.

Out in the courtyard pool, bobbing and rolling gently at the bottom of the shallow end, was a round object the size of a soccer ball. It was surrounded by murky water of a considerably darker hue than the light blue elsewhere in the pool. At the deep end, spread-eagled and looking strangely relaxed—and with another cloud of murky water trailing from it to the area under the diving board—was an object more immediately recognizable. It was the formally clad torso of what was left of a man.

★ ★ ★ ★

CHAPTER

2

"Tim" Kawamura was the second of three children. He was five centimeters shorter than his older sister but five centimeters taller than his younger brother. He played center field on his junior high school baseball team, and wrestled as a middleweight on the high school judo team. He graduated from university ranked 201st in a class of 402.

Kawamura married the girl of his parents' choice at the age of twenty-eight years, six months. He and his wife now have exactly two children and, to keep things in balance, they are of each sex. Kawamura would rather spend his days sitting in a rowboat fishing than anything he could possibly imagine. He has seven years and ninety-two days to go until retirement at age fifty-five.

An awesome talent has dogged Tim Kawamura since his junior high school days. His special skill first displayed itself, to his own amazement, in contests in and around his native island of Kyushu. As word of his abilities spread to the main island of Honshu, Kawamura was soon packed off to appear in similar but broader contests throughout the country. Once, in 1960, he even appeared on national television. The prestige and acclaim he brought to his family and teachers was incalculable, and it led to a very tangible job offer and subsequent career in which his unique abilities are employed even today.

During the pre-Olympic months in 1964, the Olympic organizers, in coordination with the Japanese government, conducted a massive campaign to prepare the local citizenry for anticipated encounters with international visitors. People like Kawamura were in great demand.

Just out of school, he was brought to Tokyo, housed in a special dormitory, and outfitted in red slacks and a white blazer with a red sun on the breast pocket. Kawamura was one of hundreds of young men and women outfitted in red slacks and white blazers with red suns on the breast pockets. Performing well during rehearsals—that old talent again— he was given a prestigious assignment. He was christened by authorities with the name Tim (it being well-known that all foreigners called people by their given names) and entrusted with the responsibility of "Liaison Official" to the visiting United States Olympic team, specifically the javelin throwers.

When, after the Games, it was determined that Kawamura had acquitted himself particularly well—especially during a potentially disastrous misunderstanding involving the javelin throwers and their javelins, the young maidens from the International School of the Sacred Heart in Tokyo, their Mother Superior, the stunned proprietor of a beer hall in the Ginza, and a local policeman on patrol in the neighborhood—he was approached by the Police

Department with an offer of permanent employment. His assistance had been deemed to be significant, and his career was guaranteed. He was now a captain and his talent was still a special and relatively rare gift.

Tim Kawamura, in public or in private, before great crowds or small, while drunk or plain sober, was able to open his mouth and make sounds emerge in a torrent. And those sounds, apparently shaped by alien forces lurking deep in the brain's chemistry, were in mysterious but apparently well-understood . . . English!

Captain Kawamura was assigned to handle whatever it was that had happened among the foreigners at the Tokyo American Club.

★ ★ ★ ★

CHAPTER

3

"Stand back everyone. Stand back."

J.B. Culhane III had been president of the Tokyo American Club for seven weeks. The mantle of authority rested uncertainly on his beefy shoulders—his most significant action as president had been his acceptance speech, in which he announced that jackets and ties would be henceforth required for entry to the mixed grill. It had been necessary for him the following week, however, to clarify by letter to all members that the pronouncement did not apply to women. "Women should wear, er, just nice things," he later explained to the Board of Governors.

Several dozen people had rushed down to the pool area after Gordy Sparks' spectacular revelation of things amiss in the water. Another three hundred or so remained in the building, crowding for space at the windows outside the ballroom, or descending to lower floors for a better view. None of the people in the pool area gave the slightest indication of doing anything but standing back.

"Stand back," J.B. roared, "wait for the police."

J.B. Culhane III was on, by his own admission, something resembling the "fast track" in his corporation. He had worked in three of four different areas of his head office, and these assignments had been interspersed with several postings to overseas corporate hot spots. "Jack," as he was known to his close friends, was both nimble and quick, and the relative frequency of his assignments allowed him to leap over the candlesticks which had burned several of his successors.

His rise in the hierarchy of the club was nothing short of phenomenal—the timing of transfers, job-changes, and expanding career responsibilities created a vacuum at the top which J.B. rose to from his former position of house committee chairman. "It will be good for business," J.B. told his head-office supervisors after his election, "and I get to write a column in the monthly club newspaper." What he did not mention, or even notice at first, was the headache of trying to satisfy thirty-five hundred members, not counting spouses and children, from forty-four different countries.

"Let's at least get the head out," said the Frenchman at J.B.'s elbow. "We can use the pool skimmer,
I think."

In a way, it was amazing that the first question
on everyone's lips was *who* the victim was, not what
happened or why. The head was covered with white
hair that floated silkily in the murky water, but the
face remained resolutely down and out of sight.

"Or let's just poke it over to see," continued the
Frenchman.

J.B. walked to the other end of the pool, telling
people hovering against the bushes in the background to stand back, and looked at the torso. Un-
fortunately, tuxedos have a uniformity about them,
making identification without living gestures, or
heads, impossible. A large area of water around the
body was clouded by the reddish-brown fluid issuing
from the neck, and columns of the stuff were already
twisting and sinking to the bottom of the pool.

Small red and blue tubes floated like strings from
the neck of the torso, and their movement in the
softly rippling water gave an appearance of life that
was, under the circumstances, grotesque. Feeling a
sudden revulsion that must have similarly affected
poor Gordy Sparks upstairs, J.B. stepped back, took
a deep breath, and looked up at the people staring
down from the windows in the main building. The
first sounds of a siren could be heard wailing in the
distance.

"O.K.," said J.B. Culhane III to the Frenchman
standing at the shallow end, "take the pole and

nudge it over." Jack had made his second decision as club president. "Stand back everyone," he added for good measure.

J.B. watched the Frenchman gingerly prod the submerged head. It took several attempts to catch the end of the pole in the area around the ear. When the pole did catch, the nudge was too sharp. The head spun completely around, white hair revolving in a trail. A lady standing near the shallow end screamed, and her escort caught her as she fell in a faint.

J.B. wiped his forehead with his handkerchief and turned toward the white wall of the recreation building. People on the fast track, he reminded himself, should avoid swooning at all costs. A babble of concerned conversation arose behind him, mingling with the "mon Dieus" from the Frenchman.

"Excuse, please," said a voice so startlingly close that J.B. dropped his handkerchief. "My name is Tim Kawamura and I am at your service. And," he added, almost as an afterthought, "I am with the Azabu Police Department."

He and J.B. exchanged business cards and bowed to each other ever so slightly. J.B. picked up his handkerchief.

"Is something wrong here?" asked Tim Kawamura. His eyes were flicking back and forth along the length of the twenty-five meter pool. His gaze rested fractionally longer at the deep end.

"Yes, Captain Kawamura," said J.B. in his best executive voice. He had positioned the handkerchief back in his jacket pocket. "It would appear that our club general manager may have, er, passed away."

★ ★ ★ ★

CHAPTER Peter ("Call me Pete") Peterson had been, until sometime between 7:30 and 8:00 on this lovely December evening, manager of the club for nearly five years. Supervising a staff of four hundred employees in a bilingual, bicultural environment was an extraordinary challenge in itself, but coordinating their efforts against a background of continual "advice" from the board, committee chairmen, and several thousand concerned members required the patience, wisdom, and strength of Job, Solomon, and Hercules.

Pete began his career washing dishes at the Palmer House Hotel in Chicago. It was a part-time job during high school, but it led to bigger and better things on the kitchen staff until, by the time he entered college, Pete could handle most chores in the food-preparation arena to the satisfaction of any chef happening to look his way. (The sour-cream-in-the-vichyssoise episode during President Truman's visit to the hotel had *not* been his fault, Pete would swear over the years: "Someone mislabeled the container.")

Despite an abrupt departure from the Palmer House, Pete's career path was clear. He enrolled in Cornell University's hotel-management program and graduated into a string of jobs encompassing virtually every aspect of hotel and club management. He crawled around boiler room pipes in Pittsburgh, managed front desks in Cleveland, made certain the greens were mowed and watered in Tampa, and estimated occupancy rates in San Francisco. He also, in a pinch, stood in for a pastry chef in New Orleans. ("The sugar-salt difficulty happens more often than is commonly known," Pete later was heard to explain.)

By the time he was hired by the Tokyo American Club, Pete had compiled an impressive resume of assignments and had accumulated all the generally accepted awards and certificates of advanced studies necessary for management in the big leagues. Other than being banned from the kitchen ("You'd be surprised how much corn starch looks like baking powder"), Pete was given the green light by the board. He ran the thirty-five-hundred-member club, and did a very good job. He had approximately 1,750 friends, and somewhere in the neighborhood of 1,750 enemies—not counting, of course, any of his three ex-wives. Or his current widow.

★ ★ ★ ★

CHAPTER

5

Agatha Christie, Michael Innes, Ngaio Marsh, Dorothy Sayers, Freeman Willis Crofts and others in the classic British detective genre would somehow contrive to assemble all suspects in the same room, or set of rooms, and "take statements."

A ham-fisted, canine-loyal, happily-married-to-someone-named-Bess-who-was-always-good-for-a-late-night-plate-of-eggs-and-tea assistant would take copious notes with the stub of a pencil that he'd lick between sentences.

The notes would be reviewed—chapters of them—by the inspector and his assistant upon the conclusion of the interviews. Turns of phrases, little lapses in alibis, and sudden emotional tics would be carefully scrutinized. ("Poppycock, my good fellow," said the man with powder burns on his wrist who claimed to be out walking the dogs alone when all the nasty business was occurring. "I *loved* my evil damn stepmother.")

Tim Kawamura's mother had been given a collection of dog-eared British mystery books by the U.S. Army Occupation officer who was billeted briefly with the Kawamuras immediately after the war. In support of his burgeoning linguistic talents, Tim had devoured the stories in his youth and had become the first in his circle of junior high school friends to employ the expletive "drat." (Once, during a speech contest, he was able to work in the words "circumstantial" and "evidence," sending the judges scurrying to their dictionaries. He won that contest.)

Experience on the police force had taught Tim that crime in real life, or at least crime outside England, was never as neat as that depicted in his treasured stories. A great deal more random violence was involved, and the real or imagined slights of forebears toward each other rarely carried through the generations to the present. ("Had your grandfather not been the bastard son of Lord Harley and his scullery maid, Great Aunt Margaret, *I'd* be Squire of Wormsley." Bang!)

And the simple test-formula of "motive, means and opportunity" never really applied, at least in Japan. Motives, of course, are universal. Problems with love, or a lack thereof, top the list, followed by issues involving money, reputation, and retribution.

But the "means" element in the formula rarely if ever included guns and automatic weaponry, with all the attendant technology of ballistics, trajectory, and calibration. In Japan only criminals possessed guns, and they shot only each other with them. Real crime largely depended on baseball bats and kitchen knives—instruments of mayhem somewhat difficult to trace.

As for the "opportunity" element, in a nation where the equivalent of half the U.S. population exists in habitable space the equivalent of the flat parts of southern California—and all rub elbows at some time or other during the day or night—lack of opportunity was impossibly impossible. Paper walls could be walked through, and frequently were.

Still, the basic principles of detection, as exemplified in the heroics of Miss Marple, Hercule Poirot, Lord Peter Wimsey, Sir John Appleby, and Inspector Alleyn, would have to be applied. If he had learned nothing else in all his years on the police force, Tim Kawamura had at least mastered the art of individual interrogation.

"I think," he said to club president J.B. Culhane III, "you should make everyone go back inside."

"Everyone? Christ, there must be . . ."

"Everyone," interrupted Kawamura. "And that includes all employees."

"But there must be close to five hundred people all together . . ."

"It will be my pleasure," continued the detective, "to interview all of them."

★ ★ ★ ★

CHAPTER

6

"The ambassadors go first," J.B. shouted into the microphone on the ballroom stage. "Stand back, the ambassadors go first."

Surprisingly, most people had allowed themselves to be led back up to the fourth-floor ballroom. Docile compliance was perhaps supported by intense curiosity as to what the hell was going on. The rumor that Pete Peterson was the man in the pool was confirmed by J.B. in his opening remarks on the stage.

"It seems," J.B. said, "that an accident has befallen our general manager, Mr. Peterson. The police wish to ask a question or two. I am authorized to advise you all to comply with this request."

Not everyone had agreed to return to the fourth floor however. The Russian ambassador—a surprise attendee at the gala ball—slipped with his entourage around the wall and into his compound. Glasnost notwithstanding, he was better off getting clear of the American Club with a developing situation certain to attract publicity and perhaps result in considerable embarrassment.

The American ambassador and his wife had also been driven from the scene immediately. The diplomatic license plates on the black limousine froze the policemen assigned by Kawamura to guard the entrance to the club. They saluted the retreating red tail lights.

Four other ambassadors did return to the ballroom. The governmental representatives of Canada, Australia, Mexico, and Pakistan pushed with their wives through the crowd to the stage.

"Stand back, everyone," boomed J.B., "and let the, er, honorable dignitaries through."

Kawamura had arranged to borrow a dressing room immediately offstage. There he positioned three of his subordinates who he knew had a basic command of English, and instructed them to obtain everyone's name, address, and a brief statement of activities since arriving at the club.

The subordinates sat behind a long table that normally served as a repository for random props and make-up kits. They spread out their papers, positioned lighters, cigarettes, and ashtrays, uncapped their pens, rolled up their sleeves, and began the familiar and very comfortable process of bureaucratic questioning. Among themselves, they agreed to each ask every guest the same three questions. The theory was that taking notes in English was

tricky enough on the face of things, and three separate stabs at the three questions would produce at
least a fairly representative composite which could
be sorted out later.

It was observed that the guests began to lose
patience with the second set of three questions, and
more particularly with the third set of three questions. Kawamura's subordinates solved the problem
by rotating themselves so that each spent time in the
second and third chairs.

Meanwhile, Kawamura prowled the pool area as
forensic experts and related scientists examined the
scene of the crime. The body and head had already
been whisked away to the police morgue where,
among other things, the cause of death would be
determined.

The fingerprint wizards in white gloves asked
Kawamura permission to leave after about an hour
on the job. They had covered about a quarter of the
area and had already lifted over two thousand prints.
It was determined, after a ten-minute conference,
that other clues would have to be found if this puzzle
was to be solved. Someone suggested draining the
pool, and a patrol was sent to try and find the location
of valves.

A breakthrough of sorts was discovered by one of
Kawamura's trainees, who was assigned to the pe-
ripheral regions of the scene. Wandering around the
kiddy pool and peering into the snack bar facilities
on the patio, he noticed a laundry cart half full of
towels. He began to rummage through the cart, and

then he noticed that the towels were stained with blood. The means of transport to the pool of the head or body, or both, was now clear. Investigation shifted focus to the snack-bar area.

J.B. spent the intervening time roaming back and forth between the third and fourth floors of the main building. The employees, some two hundred of them that evening, had been ensconced on the third floor in various banquet rooms; their turn to be interviewed would come only after the members and guests had had theirs. Chatting with the employees still awake, J.B. gradually became aware that now, without the general manager, he was *really* in charge. Someone asked him if the club would open in the morning, and J.B. realized he wasn't even certain if the club *ever* opened in the morning. "Yes," he answered, figuring the odds at roughly the same as a coin flip. "Unless we don't open," he added as a hedge.

On the fourth floor, anarchy appeared imminent. Pete's widow had made her statement (thrice) immediately after the ambassadors, and had been led down to her apartment on the B-3 level of the building for sedation and rest. Arrangements had been made by the police department to borrow a young woman from the fire department to sit with Mrs. Peterson in her grief.

Upstairs, meanwhile, the effects of shock and horror were beginning to wear off. Certainly no one was larking about, but a party *had* been going on, a great deal of alcohol *had* been consumed, and now prema-

ture hangovers and mood swings related to fluctu-
ating alcohol levels were beginning to exhibit themselves.

"Goddamit, J.B.," said the club secretary, "the
Pakistan ambassador won't go home. He keeps pushing into line to report more details of his evening's
activities to the police. He's been up there three
times."

"J.B., I'm due to catch a plane to Korea tomorrow,"
announced a young man with an excessively frilled
dress-shirt," and if I'm not out of here soon, I'm
holding you responsible."

"I say, Culhane old chap, form and all that sort of
thing are frightfully important, frightfully important indeed." The accoster was wearing medals on
his tuxedo jacket. "But I'd be ever so grateful if you'd
pop me ahead in line. My da—, ah, business associate
here is concerned about her elderly parents, getting
home and all that, and of course my wife is waiting,
well you know, frightful evening, swimming pool and
that sort of thing."

"Jacques," said Jacques, "my wife is going to have
a babee. A babeeee," he emphasized (though Mrs.
Jacques was perhaps three, three-and-a-half
months pregnant.)

"Mr. Culhane, this is my boss and his wife visiting
from Boston. They don't want to stay here any
longer."

"Hey J.B., you bloody twit, if we're not out of here
by midnight, you and Pete will soon be practicing
chord progressions together on the bloody harp."

One of the problems, J.B. noticed, was that there was, in fact, a tendency toward volubility among people involved in official inquiries. To be on the safe side, folks were telling more than the inspectors probably wanted to know. Carrying the title of "president"—a carte blanche position in Japan—J.B. was able to wander at will in and out of the interview room.

Women tended to detail trips to the ladies room, men recounted bouts of table-hopping. Gordy Sparks began rambling on about a bug in his lunch, the Pakistan ambassador described his trip to the front desk for a cigar. The inspectors would periodically hop about switching chairs, lighters, and cigarettes—Americans demanded the opportunity to consult with their lawyers. By 11:30 p.m., there were still fifty or sixty people waiting to be interviewed.

J.B. went downstairs looking for his new pal Tim.

★ ★ ★ ★

CHAPTER

7

"We think we know how Pete was murdered," confided Captain Kawamura to J.B. "Your chef informed to us that one knife and one, how you say . . . ," Kawamura made a quick chopping motion with his hand.

"Cleaver?"

"Creaver."

"Cleaver."

"Cleaver is missing."

The two men were standing in a small room off the corridor leading to the service elevator. The room was a temporary holding area for the service carts used to bring food from the B-1 main kitchen level to the banquet area on the top floors. The room was now empty except for two carts with broken wheels and a jumbled pile of large silver serving trays and domed lids in one corner.

"And that," continued Kawamura, pointing to brownish stains on the lower wall next to the room's entrance, "is blood."

J.B. and the police captain looked at the stains. Clearly, something had been splattered on the wall—almost as if a ripe tomato had been thrown against it at point-blank range.

"Are you sure? I mean, are you sure it's blood?" asked J.B. "It could be some kind of food like . . . a tomato."

"Or pumpkin?" suggested Kawamura, bringing to two the items neither man would be comfortable eating again.

"Yes, or a . . . well, never mind."

"It is no doubting blood," said Kawamura. "Those scrape marks came from our men's investigation. They have the way to judge."

"But if that's the case, how could what must have happened here really happen?"

"You mean cutting off of the head?"

"I guess so. I mean, there must be constant activity in here and out by the elevator. I don't see how such an . . . an accident . . . "

"Cutting off of the head."

" . . . could go undetected."

"According to your chef, who is by the way a Spanish," said Kawamura, "elevator is a very busy place when food goes up and plates come down."

"That's what I mean. How could . . ."

"But in between," continued Kawamura, "no business is here."

"That means that . . . er, what must have happened here . . ."

"Cutting off of the head."

"Yes, must have happened while everyone was eating food upstairs."

J.B. tried to remember if he had seen Pete during the meal. With the welcoming speech, the raising and dimming of lights, the shuffling of late-arriving people, and the general commotion attendant with serving 350 meals all at once, Culhane realized that he couldn't even begin to pin down Pete's movements. He always seemed to be around, and then he wasn't.

"But there is strange thing," said Kawamura. "Your chef who is a Spanish said no one absolutely saw Pete down here."

"But surely, there must have been people from the kitchen wandering around the hallway, or something. Obviously Pete was here," said J.B. looking at the stain on the wall.

"That is not your Spanish chef's idea."

"How can he be certain?"

"Because," said Kawamura, "he made a strict instruction for everyone to tell to him *if* Pete comes here."

"And . . . ?"

"No one told to him."

"I see."

"Because," said Kawamura, turning from the doorway and walking over to the stain on the wall, "your chef who is a Spanish said if Pete comes here, he will hit him with a . . . ," the captain made a chopping motion with his hand.

"A cleaver?"

"A cleaver."

"I see," said J.B.

★ ★ ★ ★

CHAPTER

8

It was 2:30 in the morning when the interviews with the members, guests, and employees were finally over. J.B. sat with Kawamura in the nearly deserted ballroom and reviewed the lists. It was clear that the mass of information would have to be broken down and put on a computer if any sense was to be made of it.

Various plainclothes investigators and uniformed officers wandered in and out of the room delivering brief spurts of information to Kawamura, who took their intelligence with stoicism and apparent unconcern. Photographers, for some reason, were popping their flashbulbs around the dance floor, their chores at poolside and in the kitchen now finished.

J.B. and Kawamura were joined by Gordy Sparks, whose practical role in the affair seemed clear-cut and marginal, but whose official role, Discoverer of the Body—albeit from a height of four stories—was deemed significant. They were also joined by Butch Percy, the recreation director, who was judged to have been the last person too see Pete in the ballroom. The two men and their wives had shared a table near the side entrance.

"He was up and down a lot," reported Butch, "in fact I don't think he sat down for more than five minutes during the first half hour."

"What was he doing?" asked Kawamura yawning. "I mean, where did he go up and down?"

"He went, well, I don't know exactly, just everywhere to make certain arrangements were OK, and, like that."

"You stated earlier," Kawamura read from a crumpled note, "that you last saw him just before the soup was served."

"That's right."

"What happened?"

"He said, 'Excuse me.' "

"He said, 'Excuse me?' " asked J.B., puzzled.

"I'll handle this, Culhane-san."

"Call me J.B."

"Call me Tim."

"Good, I've been calling you different names all night."

"Ahem, he said, 'Excuse me?' " asked Kawamura, turning back to Butch.

"Yes, someone came up and whispered something to him. He said 'Excuse me,' got up, and left the table."

"Who was it?" asked Gordy suddenly.

"I'll handle this, Sparks-san."

"Call me Gordy."

"Call me Captain Kawamura. Who was it?"

"I don't know. I didn't even turn around and look. It was a man, I saw the arm of a tuxedo, and," Butch yawned, "that's all."

"It was about 7:30?"

"It was about 7:30."

Another policeman approached Kawamura, muttered a few sentences and Kawamura muttered a few back. The policeman walked toward the rear of the room and out the door.

"He said the autopsy report is being delivered in a few minutes."

"Autopsy report? I would have thought, I mean even from where I was standing," said Gordy, "that . . ."

"I know," said Kawamura, stifling a yawn, "but it makes things official."

"You know Tim," announced J.B., pausing to yawn, "I've been looking at this list your men made. A number of people I know were here tonight and they aren't on the list. Is it possible your men didn't question them all?"

"Impossible," stated Kawamura. "Isn't it?"

"Actually, a number of people, mostly those who went down to the pool area, left the club property through the back gate," said Butch. "My wife was one of them."

"You mean to say," said Kawamura, turning to look back in the direction of the interrogation room next to the stage, "that all the lists we made . . . ?"

"I'm afraid so," said J.B. through the tail end of a yawn.

Kawamura threw his pencil on the table, slumped back in his chair, and closed his eyes. He opened them once to see J.B., Sparks, and Percy yawning, and closed them again. He was in the middle of a yawn of his own when a policeman with an official-looking document approached.

Kawamura looked up at the policeman after reading the document once. He looked at J.B. after reading the document a second time. He got up, walked around the table, and sat down again after reading it a third time.

"We have big mystery here at this club, J.B." said Kawamura reading the document a fourth time.

"You're telling me. Old Pete down there . . ."

"No, I mean *big* mystery," interrupted Kawamura. "What . . . ?"

"To be exact, the head does not fit on the body."

"But that's imposs . . ."

"The body," continued Kawamura, "is Japanese."

★ ★ ★ ★

CHAPTER

9

Molecular biologists are learning more every year about the genetic code found in each human cell. The code, or DNA, which is in a part of the human cell called the mitochondrion, is particularly fascinating because it is inherited only from the mother. It is postulated that humans, as we know and love ourselves today (as opposed to the earlier Neanderthal, Homo erectus, and Homo habilis models), originated in Africa more than seventy thousand years ago, gradually migrated outward to the Middle East, then Europe, and finally the Far East, Australia, and America.

The theory, and it is still a theory, maintains that modern Homo sapiens developed in parallel with the older and certainly very worthy creatures, and that the development of modern man can be traced through the DNA connection to a single human, "Eve," who was found to have lived in Africa some two hundred thousand years ago.

Tens of thousands of years of adapting to the demands of the environment have created secondary physical characteristics distinguishing races as statistical groups, but due to numerous variations, the distinctions on an individual basis are not always so readily apparent. Under the skin, all humans *are* brothers. And Japanese skin is about as "yellow" as Caucasian skin is really "white."

J.B. Culhane's reflections on the matter were substantially less profound, however. It had never occurred to him that physical indicators beneath the head might have to be employed to sort out the thorny issues implicit in this particular racial situation. One heard rumors, of course, but an element of science must be involved.

J.B. stopped his new friend as they were about to enter their cars in the club parking lot. The sky in the east was beginning to glow with the new light of day.

"Can I ask you something, Tim?"

"Certainly J.B."

"First of all, you're certain that, er, Pete's head doesn't fit on that body?"

"We're certain, J.B. The neck wounds on both parts were made by different instruments. In addition, the head doesn't fit on the body. It's, ah, technical, J.B."

"I understand, Tim. But my real question, I mean, you don't have to answer it, but . . ."

"But what?"

"Well, if you don't mind telling me."

"I can't know until you ask," said Tim getting into his car. "What?"

"Well," said J.B., clearing his throat, "what exactly, or should I say, what approximately, er, how do you know the body is actually Japanese?"

"It's easy," said Tim, signaling his driver to start. "His wallet was in his pocket."

★ ★ ★ ★

CHAPTER

10

The Tokyo American Club was founded in 1928 by a group of American and Japanese businessmen interested in establishing for themselves a facility for family dining and social intercourse. Americans were by no means the first foreign contingent of merchants and traders in Japan, but by the 1920s they were the largest. Oil companies, business-machine manufacturers, and banks were increasingly involved in successful ventures in the country, and the new American executives often arrived in Tokyo with wives and children.

The club was originally located in the old Imperial Hotel, an architectural wonder (it did not collapse during the Great Kanto Earthquake of 1923) designed by Frank Lloyd Wright. An indication of the modest circumstances surrounding the club's early operation is the fact that the twenty-three original members were each obliged to donate two chairs along with their incorporation fees. Dining and social intercourse was necessarily limited to the first forty-six people signing up for the scheduled festivities.

A major attraction at the club during the early years—major because Americans could not live without it and Japanese could not obtain it elsewhere—was the presence of meat on the menu. Shipped frozen from the States, steaks and chops were crucial to the club's success. The first recorded club employee, biculturally named Walter Watanabe, had as his duties "sweeping the floor, locking and unlocking doors, guarding the liquor, fixing the lights, and cooking the food carefully."

By the late 1930s, the club had established its own premises in an old office building near the hotel and had grown to several hundred members. Diplomats and newspapermen from over a dozen countries joined the Japanese and American businessmen in dining and social intercourse. Walter Watanabe became only one of thirteen employees on the payroll, and his responsibilities had shrunk to "keeping the billiard room neat at all times." The chef was listed as being Monsieur Adachi, and his job description omitted the adjective "carefully." He was merely charged with the responsibility of "cooking the food."

Later, suspicions that the club harbored spies, malcontents, revolutionaries, anti-militarists, seditionists, oppressors, fifth columnists, appeasers, constitutional democrats, and folks without a sense of humor about world affairs had gradually diminished the pleasure of the dining and social intercourse. (It seems that *both* Walter Watanabe and Monsieur Adachi had been drafted—their names disappeared from the roster.) Discretion being the better part of valor, the organization ceased operation during the 1941-45 misunderstanding.

In 1946, three Japanese attorneys—prewar members—popped up and presented the U.S. Occupation authorities with documents relating to the original club charter. The last prewar club president, older and definitely wiser, was prevailed upon to become the first postwar president. By 1947 the organization was off and running again. But the scope of operations rapidly surpassed anything that the collective imagination of the founders with the forty-six chairs might have conjured.

Today the club occupies several acres of its own land in a Beverly Hills-Park Avenue-Nob Hill equivalent of central Tokyo. The membership of thirty-five hundred hails from forty-four countries and totals, counting spouses and dependents, about eleven thousand individuals.

The organization runs thirty-eight adult-education classes and arranges tours all over Asia. There are youth activity programs, including baseball, soccer, basketball, swimming, and scouting. Hundreds of formal and informal business meetings occur at the club each week—about half the two thousand meals served each day in the six dining facilities are in the expense-account category. A successful candidate for the presidency of the United States initially announced his availability in the club—and a prime minister of Japan successfully announced his resignation in the club. And as confirmation of the role played by the organization at the core of the members' lives, the videotape library averages over a quarter-million checkouts each year.

Yet despite its humble beginnings, its checkered early history, a cook named Walter, its accidental position next to the Russian Embassy, the potpourri of membership, and the rogues galley of organizational geniuses, dedicated public servants, buffoons and madmen at the helm, the club had never dealt with a situation such as that currently at hand. No one, at least as far as records indicate, had ever whacked off the general manager's head and deposited it, along with an unidentified Japanese body, in the club swimming pool. (But then again, the pool wasn't built until 1974, and Walter's whereabouts remain unknown.)

★ ★ ★ ★

CHAPTER

11

Angie Peterson awoke with a funny taste in her mouth and the chill of a horrible nightmare still tingling just below her consciousness. The low winter sun was streaming in the window and across her blanket. That's strange, she thought, Pete always closes the shades before going to bed. Stranger yet, the blanket was only used on the very coldest of nights. Rolling onto her stomach she realized that she was still wearing her brassiere. What on earth?

The pile of clothes in the armchair next to the bed suddenly moved. Wait a minute. Angie sat up, squinted her eyes into focus, and recognized the sleeping young lady from the night before. It was true. Good God, the dream was true. She howled, the young lady howled, and the next half hour was lost in a maelstrom of hysteria.

Angie and Pete had been married six years. Pete's first wife, a waitress at the Palmer House Hotel, was the mother of Peter Junior. He was born four months after the wedding and had enjoyed a stable family life for approximately six months. Pete's first child, now age forty, was one year older than Angie. Pete had only seen his first-born a half dozen times down through the years, and he had not seen his first wife, he maintained, since the day of the divorce.

Pete's second marriage lasted seventeen years and produced two daughters, both now married, who were the pride and joy of his life. Both had visited Japan within the last two years, both adored Angie, and both considered their father to be the finest human being on the planet. Their mother, to everyone's complete amazement, had suddenly picked up one day and walked out on the family and into the arms of a Swiss maitre d' employed by Pete at the Philadelphia Cricket Club. She still sent Christmas cards from Switzerland each year and, though divorced, still used the name Peterson.

Pete's third wife was a colossal mistake. Reeling from the shock of losing his helpmate of nearly two decades to a "yodeling gigolo," and traumatized by the prospect of raising two teenage daughters alone, he married a woman named Kate early one morning during a Club Managers of America convention in Las Vegas. The next day Pete helped the woman named Kate pack for the trip back to Philadelphia, got her on the plane, and got her off the plane in Philadelphia and to the club. The morning after that, Pete again helped the woman named Kate pack, got her on the plane, and never saw her again. As part of that divorce settlement he agreed to make child-support payments to an offspring he couldn't remember siring.

Angie met Pete in her bank. He would come into the bank once a week, and as the months went by he would manage more often than not to visit her teller's window. When the bank adopted the "express line" concept, the choreography of "timing" became crucial. Angie would stall customers at her window—counting and recounting bills—until Pete hit the front of the line. Her "next" would then ring loud and true.

Pete was considerably older, Angie knew, but he was good-natured and seemed quite virile in a mature and intriguing way. Her first husband, from whom she was divorced long before Pete began coming to her bank, had been a high-school classmate from Scranton. He and Angie graduated from school, and from going steady to marriage, on the same day.

Although Angie and her first husband had been married ten years, virility and maturity were not attributes he had brought to the relationship. It was as if, Angie came to realize, he had stopped growing and would always remain a nineteen-year-old. His interests were confined to playing softball in the industrial league for machine-shop employers, and hanging around the neighborhood bar before and after the games. He and Angie spent time together, of course, but drinking beer in the car at outdoor movies had its social limitations. Without really knowing what it was, Angie began to believe that there was something better for her in life. She left her husband and started the search for something better the day he came home with a wedding anniversary present for her—a tattoo on his arm that said "Angie."

Angie and Pete dated for nearly eight months, and Pete proposed marriage slightly over six years ago during a Thanksgiving party at the club he was managing. The flowers, champagne, diamond ring, and whispered endearments were touches of class that overwhelmed the girl who had spent so many wasted hours at drive-ins. Angie accepted the proposal with only one small worry—that Pete thought she, né Angela Garcia, was a blonde.

Today, in fact, would have been their sixth anniversary. Angie flopped back onto the bed and gave in to another bout of hysteria.

★ ★ ★ ★

CHAPTER

12

"It's a big place," Tim Kawamura reported to the Chief of the Azabu Police Department at the 8:00 a.m. meeting. "There are four floors above ground, but five floors below ground. The club is built on the side of a hill."

"You had over thirty men there last night. I can't imagine that you couldn't spare a few of them to search the buildings."

"That's of course true, Chief, and I certainly," said Kawamura, "admit failure on that crucial point. But it wasn't until almost everyone had left that we knew there was a second body." or, I should say, second body and second head."

Chief Arai was a large man who tended to use his size as a weapon to intimidate in face-to-face encounters. Originally from the northern island of Hokkaido, it was rumored that Arai was part Russian, at least on his mother's side, and that in his youth he would amuse himself and stun his neighbors by picking up his playmates and throwing them across the road or over small buildings.

"You," Chief Arai bellowed down and about the head and shoulders of Kawamura, "take thirty men and go back to that club and stay there until we get some answers. I have to report to the ward office, the Tokyo city government, the Foreign Ministry, and the Diet. And they just think a foreigner's involved. Wait until the evening papers come out and reveal that the body of one of *us* is also involved. That makes it international!"

"Yes sir," said Kawamura, bowing and backing from the room. "Your advice as always is perfectly correct."

Returning to his corner cubicle one floor below the chief's office, Tim Kawamura gathered his senior staff plus the other detectives involved in the "American Club thing" and began the ordeal of reviewing what was known and what was not. A half-dozen or so of his advisers were already occupying all the flat surfaces in his room, and another four or five—continual movement in and out the door kept the number in flux—perched on the edge of windowsills or leaned against filing cabinets.

"How long can we keep the club closed?" asked one of the sergeants, who had distinguished himself the previous evening by finding the valves that drained the pool. The sudden and unscheduled release of 185,000 gallons of water into the neighborhood sewage system had created spectacular flooding problems in the shops and houses at the bottom of the hill below the club. The reports on this episode, filed in triplicate by both the Department of Water and Department of Health, had yet to reach Chief Arai's desk.

"As long as we wish," answered Kawamura. "But I think we should plan on obtaining all the physical evidence today—it is Arai-san's fervent wish."

The men in the office grumbled assent as they shifted position, moved knees, and squeezed even closer together. Two tea girls in identical blue shifts and white blouses were now in the room distributing the steaming green liquid. They were followed by three fingerprint experts who brought chairs from the outer office and placed them in the doorway, trapping the tea girls inside. (The tea girls stood demurely against the windows for the duration of the meeting—empty trays clasped to their groins.)

"Let's first review all the relevant facts," suggested Kawamura. "It appears there were two murders and at least one of them occurred between the time the general manager was last seen at 7:30 and when his body—or excuse me, his head—was discovered at 8:00 in the pool."

Everyone nodded in agreement.

"And we have not recovered his body, but we can assume it's still on the premises," continued Kawamura.

Everyone nodded in agreement.

"We also know that the body in the pool belonged to someone named Yoshio Endo of Yokohama—at least that's what the identification in his pocket said."

Everyone nodded in agreement.

"And we don't have that body's head."

Everyone nodded in agreement. Kawamura stood up, paced the one step that the space in the room allowed, then sat down.

"Have we confirmed the identity of that body?" asked Kawamura.

"Yes," replied one of the fingerprinters. "And we confirmed his prints with his employers."

Kawamura looked up at the man. Although non-Japanese residents are mandatorily fingerprinted, Japanese rarely are, unless they have criminal records.

"His employers maintained records for everyone working there," continued the fingerprinters.

"Where?" asked Kawamura.

"Next-door," answered the man.

"Next-door to the police station?"

"No, next-door to the club," said the man. "The Russian embassy," he added.

Kawamura again rose from his chair, paced the one step back and forth for nearly a minute, and returned to his seat.

"Are you certain, I mean, that he works for the Russian embassy?"

"Yes, certain," said the fingerprint expert. "And the funny thing is that he was not invited to the party—in fact no one can imagine why he was there in formal dress. He was only a security guard."

Kawamura gazed at the man in silence, then shifted his eyes to the ceiling of his office.

"I will have to inform Chief Arai of this new development," he announced finally. "Then we will go to the club and find the other head, and the other body."

★ ★ ★ ★

CHAPTER

13

Chef Juan Carlos Garcia y Maria Elena Baez Quinn's father and grandfather were reputed to have made the best chorizos in all of Barcelona. As a little boy, Juan Carlos would often help his elders prepare the scraps of meat, flesh, and bones which would be fed into the grinder as part of the sausage making process.

His grandfather's grinder was an old, hand-cranked model that stood in a room next to the freezer at the rear of the family butcher shop. Juan Carlos would be allowed to turn the crank ("slowly, young man, slowly," his grandfather would say) while the old man carefully examined the product of the exercise as it oozed through the five holes in the grinder's spigot.

It wasn't until Juan Carlos was in his early teens that his grandfather revealed the "secret of spicing" which made the family sausage so widely popular. He would carefully watch his grandfather sprinkle, almost lovingly, the red and green peppers, the three different grinds of black pepper, and the other dabs and pinches of exotic herbs into the mixture at different stages in the sausage-making process.

Juan Carlos' father moved the process from the butcher shop to a large shed attached to his new restaurant in central Barcelona. He installed a large meat grinder, driven by an electric motor, which was capable of handling entire animals. The grinding gears and teeth blades were huge, and lubrication from the tank of cooking oil at the top of the machine was automatic. Spices were added to the mixture by hand-scoops having one-liter capacity. Everyone still praised the finished product, but Juan Carlos knew deep inside that the sausage made by his grandfather had been better. The old hand-cranked grinder that had belonged to his grandfather was the one special item in his culinary tool chest that had made the trip to Japan when Juan Carlos accepted the position of Tokyo American Club chef.

And the members were always pleased when Juan Carlos found time to crank out his little specialty.

"Those fools think I did it to Pete," Juan Carlos explained to his wife Yasuko at breakfast. Yasuko and Juan Carlos had met and married in Honolulu where they were both working for that fine old Japanese establishment, the Royal Hawaiian Hotel.

"In fact," he went on, "I'm a suspect!"

"Please not to be excited," soothed Yasuko. Having lived with Juan Carlos for seven years, she knew he was not at his best when he threw pots and pans around the room, ripped off his chef's hat and jacket and stomped on them, or swung knives and cleavers in the air over his head. People tended to misunderstand his sensitivities in those circumstances.

"I go to the club to meet the police at 9:00. If they do not believe me, then I choke them with my own hands," Juan Carlos demonstrated by crushing a loaf of bread, "and throw *them,*" he said, tossing the bread out the eighth-floor window of their apartment, "in the pool."

"OK," said Yasuko, "but please not to be excited."

"I will be a picture of calm in front of those pigs," Juan Carlos assured her. "Give me some more bread before I go."

"You, ah . . . we have no more bread, Juan Carlos."

"Impossible to live with no bread," Juan Carlos mumbled to himself as he put on his coat and shoes at the front door. An old soup spoon served as a shoehorn in the household.

"By the way, Yasuko," Juan Carlos announced with his hand on the doorknob, "I'll be bringing home some of my sausage for dinner."

★ ★ ★ ★

CHAPTER

14

Without Mrs. Takeshita's active involvement in club affairs, the place would fall apart. Or, at the very best, barely hang together.

As manager of the Housekeeping Department, Mrs. Takeshita ran a squadron of cleaning ladies with the efficiency and control of the most dedicated drill sergeant. Presidents, board members, and club managers came and went, and of course, the club members came and went. But Mrs. Takeshita had always been there, in fact her first day of work had been the day the club moved to its present location on December 15, 1954. She cleaned up after the opening ceremonies.

Mrs. Takeshita's squadron was responsible not only for maintaining spotless conditions in the public areas, but also for keeping the "backstairs" area of the buildings neat and orderly. That was the less glamorous aspect of the job, particularly on mornings after late-night dances and parties when the waiters and busboys tended to leave things where they lay in their mad dash to catch the last trains home.

It was because of the extra work involved with cleaning up after late-night parties that Mrs. Takeshita always went to the club early the following morning. The extra half hour before anyone else arrived was the ideal time to walk around and make note of the more spectacular results of the havoc wrought at these functions, and to prepare in her mind the required cleaning assignments.

As she approached the building on this particular Saturday morning, Mrs. Takeshita noticed that more than the normal number of uniformed policemen were standing around with wires in their ears, but she assumed it either had something to do with demonstrations scheduled for later in the day at the Russian Embassy or perhaps the fact that the little shops and houses at the bottom of the hill seemed to have been hit by a flash flood of some kind during the night. Mrs. Takeshita, in fact, had to skirt her way around a tidy little lake that had formed outside the "love hotel," climb the hill to the club, and enter via the employees' entrance. That was no problem, however. As head cleaning lady, Mrs. Takeshita knew more about the building than anyone. And she knew that the rusty door next to the loading ramp was never locked—the key had been missing since December 16, 1954.

Inside the club, Mrs. Takeshita checked the public areas first. It was not unusual to find members, the morning after evening festivities, asleep on isolated couches, under tables, or slumped disgracefully in and around the toilet facilities. One of the members of her squadron had early one morning discovered the fancy man, who was now president of the club, babbling incoherently to his reflection in the washroom mirror as he stood at the sink scrubbing his hands over and over again. The opinion among the cleaning ladies was that the fancy man had been making up for all the other times he used the facilities and ignored the washing phase.

Mrs. Takeshita, satisfied that no members had remained overnight in an incapacitated state, went down the service elevator to the kitchen area. Someone had taped a pink ribbon across the entrance to the little room next to the elevator, and this, Mrs. Takeshita knew, would not do. The busboys were always dumping the domed serving tray lids in the corner of the room, and their paraphernalia cluttered the space favored by the cleaning ladies for storing their mops and buckets. She had complained to the chef before, and she would certainly complain again. Mrs. Takeshita strode with purpose through the tape and walked over to inspect her buckets under the pile of lids.

* * * *

"That lady in there has something to show you sir," said one of the uniformed policemen guarding the club's front doors. Tim Kawamura and his senior investigators had just gotten out of their cars. "And she won't show it to anyone but the man in charge."

"What's she doing inside the club?" asked Tim. "Weren't your people guarding it?"

"She said it was none of our business how she got into the club," said the policeman, "in fact she has been trying to order our people out."

Kawamura walked up the steps to the large glass doors and entered the building. Planted squarely center lobby was Mrs. Takeshita. At her feet was a ordinary cleaning bucket or pail. She had placed a domed lid from a serving tray on top of the bucket.

Kawamura and Mrs. Takeshita introduced them-selves, and in deference to her age, Tim held his bow a trifle longer than he would have otherwise. Mrs. Takeshita carefully studied the card she was given, and compared the name on the card with the black plastic name tag on his suit jacket.

"OK," she said, satisfied that all was in order. "But you must understand that I don't think there is anything amusing about this at all."

With that pronouncement, Mrs. Takeshita leaned down, grasped the serving tray lid, glanced at Kawamura, and pulled the cover away.

Looking up at one and all, from the snug depths of the cleaning bucket, was the grimacing head of Yoshio Endo.

★ ★ ★ ★

CHAPTER

15

"Why have you arrested our chef?" J.B. Culhane III asked Tim Kawamura. The two men were sitting in the general manager's office formerly belonging to Pete Peterson. "What evidence do you have that he did it?"

"Of course we have not real evidence," answered the police captain, "and we have not really arrested him. He is, how you say, volunteering to assist with our investigation."

"But taking him out of here in what looked like a straitjacket didn't appear to be, from my point of view, all that voluntary," observed J.B.

"Well, as you know, he is a Spanish . . ."

"I've confirmed that already," interrupted J.B.

"And he became, how you say, very exciting when we talked to him. In fact," Kawamura continued, "he tried to hit my sergeant over the head with an iron frying pan."

"But that's pretty much his normal style," explained J.B. "Good chefs are like artists, and artists are often temperamental. As I recall, he even chased our headwaiter around the kitchen with a chicken."

"Chickens aren't iron frying pans," commented Kawamura, looking out the window of the office.

"They can be just as lethal if they're frozen," stated J.B. after a moment's pause. "The funny thing is," he added, "when everything calmed down between him and the headwaiter, he not only apologized—he kissed the man."

"Maybe he had some problem with your general manager and things went too far. Maybe afterwards it was too late to kiss him."

"Maybe," said J.B., also looking out the window, "but for some reason I just can't imagine it."

A waiter from the club coffee shop entered the room and distributed cups, saucers, sugar, cream, and two small pots of coffee. A number of club employees had drifted in to work unaware initially of the adventures of the night before. With Kawamura's permission, J.B. maintained a skeleton staff just too keep basic services running. Members, however, were barred from the premises. J.B. watched out the window as the police, and two or three parking-lot attendants, turned away members arriving to participate in the annual "polar bear" swim event scheduled to be held in the now-empty club pool.

"I can't imagine it either," said Kawamura after the waiter left. "After we took him to our station we received the report from our staff that interviewed the kitchen employees."

"And they confirmed my opinion?" asked J.B.

"Well, I don't know about that, but they confirmed something else."

"What?" asked J.B.

"Your chef, who is a Spanish by the way, did not move from his position near the kitchen doors all evening. He inspected, as the employees definitely report, every 'goddamn plate' going to the floor. He even," continued Kawamura, "put his finger in each bowl of soup to make certain it was hot enough."

"I see," said J.B., looking at his cup of coffee.

"We will be releasing your Spanish chef within the hour," said Kawamura.

"Good," said J.B., placing his cup back on the saucer.

★ ★ ★ ★

CHAPTER

16

Gordy and Ann Sparks lived in the Azabu Towers complex immediately adjacent to the Tokyo American Club. The Sparks' living room overlooked both the club and the Russian Embassy. From his position in his favorite easy chair, Gordy could see the window on the club's top floor from which he peered the evening before. The perspective was of course different—the apartment was on the tenth floor of the building—but the elements were the same. The only obstruction in his view of the club's property was afforded by the balcony extension of his neighbor one floor below—Gordy could only see one corner of the pool's deep end.

"Don't dwell upon this terrible thing," said Gordy's wife, coming up behind her husband and rubbing his shoulders. The couple had just finished breakfast and were still in pajamas and bathrobes. "The police will settle everything."

"I know, but the whole thing is awful," said Gordy, rising and tightening his bathrobe belt. "Something is very wrong over there."

Gordon W. Sparks had been sent to Japan three years before by the Western Association of Meat Packers, whose interest was in providing American beef to the citizens of Japan under the import quotas and guidelines in effect at the time. The idea was that restrictions on beef imports could not continue forever, and when the restrictions were eventually eased, market positioning during the hard times would pay off during the easy times.

Gordy had done his best during the three years, and had romanced every thug and gangster involved in the meat business. He made calls on the "families" controlling distribution, noting privately that ownership of the meat would change corporate hands as much as half-a-dozen times before the product ever left the warehouse. Each change in ownership brought a price increase, so that by the time a simple sirloin steak reached the consumer the cost would be several hundred percent higher than the import price. And the better cuts were ripped off somewhere along the line to boot, leaving only the bottom grades for sale as "U.S. beef."

Gordy and the Western Association of Meat Packers were now, after three years, positioned rather well. The easing of import restrictions was still being negotiated bilaterally at the highest levels of the U.S. and Japanese governments. But time was beginning to run out for Gordy. He had been sent to Japan when each dollar purchased 180 of the little yens, but now those same dollars only bought 120 of them. The pressure was on to increase meat sales and meet the increasing costs of keeping Gordy posted to Japan. Failure would mean giving up the ex-pat life and all the perks that went with it—including membership in the Tokyo American Club.

"I'm due over there at noon," said Gordy to his wife. He slipped off his robe as he walked to the bedroom. "I'm supposed to meet Culhane and that policeman to report on anything I may have seen from the fourth-floor window."

"Didn't you tell them everything last night?" Ann Sparks asked her husband.

"I'm not sure," said Gordon W. Sparks, closing the bedroom door.

CHAPTER

17

"He seems like a nice man," said Captain Kawamura's sergeant—the one in charge of the search-every-nook-and-cranny-of-the-whole-damn-place-until-the-second-headless-body-is-found detail. He and Kawamura were walking down the stairway from the B-1 kitchen level of the building to the B-2 level. "But for having an important job like being the president of this club, he doesn't know much about the physical plant."

"Mr. Culhane's only been the president for a month or two," replied Kawamura, "and I don't think the Americans have a good system for leadership succession. Look at how they choose vice presidents, for example."

The two men were descending to a basement level into which outside food and services were delivered. A corridor extended from the basement area to a large sliding door that opened onto a side street on the hill next to the club.

"He didn't even know where supplies were delivered to his place," continued the sergeant. "He must've thought they came in the main entrance along with all the members."

The sergeant chuckled at his little joke.

"You mean," said Kawamura, stopping at the bottom of the stairs while his eyes adjusted to the gloom, "that all these boxes and crates are moved through here on a regular basis?" Dozens of containers were stacked along the corridor in random piles on the floor or on wooden skids.

"Yes," answered the sergeant. "The chef told our investigators that the club serves an average of two thousand meals a day. That makes it one of the largest food operations in Japan."

Five men from the Azabu Police Department were methodically opening and searching through the contents of the containers. Many of the products had been imported from the United States, but Kawamura was impressed by the quantity of foodstuffs originating in Japan.

"Frozen goods and meat," continued the sergeant, "are moved immediately to the refrigeration room over there." The sergeant pointed down a hallway leading at right angles from their present position. Several more policemen were rummaging through the refrigeration units, moving barrels and whole sides of beef in and out of the freezers. "And the food in there turns over every forty-eight hours."

"Amazing," said Kawamura, walking along the corridor leading to the outside doors. "The Americans seem to have organized things better than I thought."

"And here," said the sergeant, pointing to a rusty metal door next to the large entranceway, "is where Mrs. Takeshita entered the club earlier today. As you can see, this lock hasn't been used for years."

Kawamura and the sergeant stood on the narrow loading platform and looked up and down the street. Large apartment buildings lined the opposite side, but the club side was a mass of enormous stones forming a wall two stories high. Immediately uphill from where they stood was an identical service entrance, also with a small and equally rusty door.

"Does that belong to the club too?" asked Kawamura, pointing uphill.

"No, that is the entrance to the Russian Embassy service area," answered the sergeant. "The two properties come together right here, and it seems that the entrances through the wall were built at the same time."

Kawamura and the sergeant were standing in the street looking at the twin apertures when one of the searchers from inside appeared in the doorway.

"I think we found one of the murder weapons," he announced matter-of-factly. He was blowing on his hand through bluish lips, an indication of where his assignment had been. "At the rear of the meat freezer was a . . . " The man made a chopping motion with his hand.

"Cleaver?" suggested Kawamura.

"Cleaver," agreed the policeman. "And it matches the description of the one missing from the kitchen. It has the chef's name engraved on it."

★ ★ ★ ★

CHAPTER

18

"I told you never to visit me here. And now is the worst time of all."

Angie Peterson had spent the last hour, after the woman from the Fire Department left, pacing back and forth in the living room of her apartment on the B-3 level of the club. The apartment was down one floor from the supply entrance and on the opposite side of the building. It overlooked the top floors of the love hotel situated at the base of the club's hill.

"But I just had to see you for a few minutes," said Angie's visitor, "to make certain you're OK."

"How can I be OK? My husband's dead, I'm stuck here by myself on the other side of the world, and I have friends like you who . . ."

"Angie, please, let's have a drink or something."

"At eleven o'clock in the morning?"

"Or a cup of coffee. Please Angie, I want to talk about what happened to Pete," said the visitor.

Angie looked at the man as he rapidly clenched and unclenched his fists not unlike a nervous eight-year-old. How could she have ever become involved with a man like this? The boredom of long hours alone while Pete was working, and the humiliation of frequent snubbings by the wives of members were factors, no doubt, but why couldn't she at least have chosen a lover with less of a tendency toward wimpishness.

"All right, sit down and I'll make some coffee. But you'll have to leave as soon as we're finished. The police inspector is coming to see me in half an hour."

"Pete was a little sick, you know," said the visitor when Angie returned from the kitchen. He was looking through the telescope Pete had mounted on the windowsill. It was focused on the love hotel. "People going to those places only want a few hours of privacy. And here was Pete spying on them."

"That didn't make him a sick man," said Angie. "He would just say it was better than television."

"Listen," said the visitor, turning to Angie, "I would like to know what you plan to tell the police when they question you."

"Tell them? I'll tell them whatever they want to know."

"You won't tell them about us, will you?"

"Of course not," replied Angie. "That has nothing to do with Pete's death. Nothing at all." She paused and looked up at her visitor. "Does it?" she added weakly.

"Don't be silly. But the police might misunderstand. It's my advice to answer all their questions with a simple yes or no."

"Look, I'm upset—this is the worst thing that's ever happened to me. My husband . . . is dead," said Angie starting to cry again, "but I'm not an idiot, I won't . . ."

"And Angie," said the visitor, interrupting, "tell the police I was in the ballroom the whole time last night."

Angie wiped her eyes and looked up at the visitor.

"But you were. At least I think so. There was so much commotion—people coming and going. Wait, I remember talking to your wife alone. Where . . . ?

"You just tell the police I was there," said the visitor.

Angie stared at the man as he rose to leave.

"You *were* gone for awhile," she said.

"I know, but trust me, Angie."

"Leave me alone now," said Angie after a moment of silence. "I want to think . . . by myself."

Butch Percy, recreation director, placed his coffee cup on the table and, walking softly, went out the door.

★ ★ ★ ★

CHAPTER

19

"I don't know where it is we are," stated Tim Kawamura to J.B. Culhane III. The two men were again seated in the club general manager's office. It was 2:00 in the afternoon.

"I interviewed Mrs. Peterson in her apartment. She could give no help why someone killed her husband. She only answered yes or no to my questions," continued Kawamura. "But my feeling is she is frightening of something."

"What?" asked J.B., suddenly becoming alert.

"I don't know."

"You don't think she's afraid someone is going to kill her? I mean, we'll get a bad reputation if too many murders happen here," said J.B.

"Reputation I think you will already get. No, I feel she is afraid for someone else. Who are her friends?"

"Well," said J.B. "I suppose her husband was, well of course he was, her friend and, er, come to think of it I don't know. She didn't mix with people very much and, er, I'm new in this job. In fact, I only met her once before last night."

"And . . . ?"

"And, that's all I know. The first time I met her was at a staff party last month. I was surprised that she was speaking to our chef in Japanese."

"Your chef is a Spanish," said Kawamura, "and my investigators think he can only say cooking words in Japanese."

"Maybe they were talking about cooking. Or," said the American Club president, "maybe they were speaking Spanish. It was one of those foreign languages. But in any event, I don't know much about her."

Kawamura looked out the window at the club parking lot. A horde of newspaper and television people were being kept at bay along with random club members apparently unaware of the continuing investigation on the premises. Lots of arm-waving and deep bowing was going on. "It sure was easier," said Kawamura, as much to himself as to J.B., "when I was a young policeman."

"It sure was easier," agreed J.B., "before I became president of this place."

"Anyway," said Kawamura, returning to the matter at hand, "I next interviewed again Mr. Sparks. I am feeling that he too is frightening of something or someone."

"Gordy? He's frightened of his own shadow. By the way, did he say something to you about eating bugs when he was little kid?"

"Yes," answered Kawamura, "but I don't know what he is talking about."

"I don't either. Sometimes he's a little strange."

"But Mr. Sparks also has strange situation," continued Kawamura. "He said he was looking out of window on fourth floor for ten minutes before he noticed the head and the body in the swimming pool. And he said he saw no one making any movement. I cannot imagine not to see something, or at least the . . . ah . . . things in the pool."

"He was probably daydreaming. Or," J.B. corrected himself, "nightdreaming. Gordy doesn't always focus."

"That must be it, but he became very nervous—in fact, I thought he was going to be sick—when I told to him that we can find no one who noticed him standing at that window for ten minutes before he discovered the . . . ah . . . head and the body."

"People often don't notice Gordy Sparks, Tim. He's one of those people."

"I guess so. By the way, J.B.," Kawamura changed the subject as he stood to pace, "does the club have any policy about hiring relatives?"

"Hiring relatives? How do I know . . . wait a minute, I do know of one set of sisters working here. We must allow it, I suppose. Why?"

"Because of Takeshita-san."

"The former prime minister?"

"No," said Kawamura, stopping and looking at J.B. "*Your* Takeshita-san."

"*My* Takeshita-san? Oh, you mean Mrs. Takeshita who found the other head?"

Kawamura returned to his chair, flopped down and loosened his necktie. He looked at his notes

— 61 —

neatly arranged on his side of the general manager's desk.

"No, I do not mean Mrs. Takeshita," he explained. "Don't you know all your people?"

"I know many of them, or at least some of them . . . er . . . at least by sight I more or less know . . . a few," said J.B.

"Well, he is one of your senior people. And he was slow to admit that it is his wife who is a cleaning lady."

"Is he a cleaning lady too? Wait . . . of course not, he can't be a cleaning lady. What does he do?"

"He's in charge of purchasing all club supplies," said Kawamura.

"Oh," observed J.B.

"And we found the second murder weapon—the knife—wrapped in a bloody shirt in his locker."

"My goodness."

"But," added Kawamura, looking up from his notes, "he was not on duty last night."

★ ★ ★ ★

CHAPTER

20

The interview at the Russian embassy was scheduled for 3:00 p.m. A Russian-speaking Japanese interpreter had been unearthed at Tokyo University by the Azabu Police Station. The man, a professor on the language faculty, explained excitedly to Captain Kawamura that after twenty years of teaching Russian, this would be his first opportunity to actually speak it to someone other than his students.

The interview would not be with the ambassador—he was tied up with higher matters of state—but it would be with his number one deputy. Charges d'Affaires Konstantin Gregoravich Borosov was authorized to respond to all inquiries about the ambassador's movements the night before at the dinner-dance, as well as to provide information relative to the embassy employee whose body spent time with Pete Peterson's head in the American Club swimming pool.

The fact that the American Club and the Russian Embassy are immediate neighbors sharing a common wall is often cited as one of the anomalies resulting from the general lack of space in Tokyo. In fact, the Russians purchased most of the land around the embassy, including the land occupied by the American Club, in the 1920s. Unbelievable as it may see, the property was at the time considered to be far enough from the downtown area to qualify as a "country retreat" for senior staff working at the original city-center embassy. When the entire embassy operation was moved to its present site in the 1930s, some of the land was sold to the Japan-based Manchurian Railway Company.

After the war, when the Americans were scouting around for suitable property to reestablish the club, the land was purchased from the trustees of the suddenly defunct railway company. The Russians were not in a position financially to reacquire the property, a situation no doubt viewed with some regret today.

The grounds of the embassy were still spacious, but the expansion in recent years of office facilities and living quarters encroached upon the original rustic ambiance. A tennis court, outdoor basketball court, and an open sports area used primarily for volleyball were still nestled among the trees, but the harsh contours of a grade-school building and a modern communication center reflected the modern requirements of one of the Soviet Unions' largest overseas enclaves.

Kawamura and the interpreter were ushered into a large conference room adjacent to the entrance hallway on the first floor of the main embassy building. It was a bit unnerving for both men to have the ushering conducted by a large-framed, full-chested blond woman with astonishingly blue eyes, and a command of impeccable Japanese. The interpreter silently held her in open-mouthed awe.

"Amazing," he said to Kawamura as soon as they were alone. "She sounds like one of us."

A minute or two later a young man of Slavic appearance entered the room and served steaming cups of black tea. To Kawamura's surprise, the young man remained in the room and chatted about the weather, traffic conditions, the yen-dollar exchange rate, teen pop singers on television, the fortunes of the Tokyo Giants baseball team, and the recent succession in the Imperial Family—all in equally impeccable Japanese.

To Tim Kawamura, winner of contests as a youth, bilingualism was something he appreciated and understood. But that was because his bilingualism had from his point of view sensible native Japanese as a base. With that base, speaking other languages was merely an elaborate parlor trick. It became just a question of memorizing words non-Japanese used to express themselves. How could anyone, he wondered, approach that sensible base language with such proficiency and yet not be Japanese? He found it difficult to look at the alien face mouthing the real words that burrowed so directly into his mind. It was a relief in a way when the blond woman returned and stated that the charges d'affaires was ready for the meeting.

Kawamura and the interpreter, who had yet to utter a word in Russian, followed the blond woman up a flight of stairs to the left of the reception area. On the second floor they walked past a number of offices which, Kawamura noted, were each occupied by four or five individuals. His first impression was that although the scene appeared similar to any ordinary business operation, the relative absence of Japanese natives and women was peculiar. Young men in shirt sleeves, like the one who served the tea, apparently handled most typing and clerical duties. Older men wearing suit jackets seemed to be the executives.

The blond woman showed the men into a large room used for formal receptions. With its ornate chandeliers, cream-colored walls, and red plush

chairs, Kawamura remarked that it reminded him
of his weekend trip to Europe the previous year and
his two-hour stop at the Palace of Versailles.

"But this is Russian," the lady explained, pointing
to a huge mosaic that entirely covered one wall of
the room. Indeed, an artist had assembled painted
pieces of metal showing a perspective of Moscow as
seen from above. "And these buildings," she continued, indicating what seemed to be dozens of onion-
spired churches, "are official state museums."

The meeting with the charges d'affaires was held
in a smaller but more richly appointed version of the
downstairs conference room. A table with space for
four chairs on each side and two at the ends dominated the room. A painting of a winter scene with
what looked like a peasant's hut surrounded by bo-
vine creatures rummaging in the snow dominated
the wall opposite the curtained windows. A tinted
black-and-white photograph of Lenin hung on the
wall at the head of the table. A highly polished but
old-fashioned samovar stood on a small side table
next to an eight-line, push-button telephone-speaker
module of space-age design. The rug on the parquet
floor was, Kawamura noted, an Afghan.

"It is so kind of you to visit us here," said Mr.
Borosov as he breezed into the room. "This is Mr.
Pushkin," he added, introducing a short, balding
man trailing behind. "He is my assistant. And this,"
he continued, indicating a tall, attractive lady, "is
Miss Torpev, the ambassador's secretary." Mr.
Borosov did not bother to mention the name of the

solid lady who also joined the group and sat in the sixth chair with her notepad.

The civility of introductions completed—a slight hitch had developed when the interpreter discovered he had forgotten his business cards, but agreed to mail them to the embassy later—Mr. Borosov stated his interest in "getting down to business." His comments were also in impeccable Japanese.

Mr. Borosov was, Kawamura thought, a pleasant man. He had a broad, open face, high forehead, and eyes that seemed to twinkle with goodwill. A jolly laugh seemed always to be lurking just beneath the surface. He included each member of his entourage in his deliberations over the questions asked of him by seeking their assent with polite little nods and bows. Seeking consensus of the group was a sensible touch not always found in foreigners, Kawamura observed.

No, the ambassador did not mention seeing anything unusual last night, but the ambassador rarely visited the American Club.

Yes, the ambassador did leave the club as soon as the unpleasantness was discovered, but then that's only natural, given his position.

No, the ambassador was not personally acquainted with the security guard, Yoshio Endo. (The ambassador's secretary, even prettier now with her glasses on, coughed slightly.) Or at least, it was explained by the charges d'affaires, the ambassador did not know the man except for perhaps a chance encounter at employees' parties at the embassy.

Yes, Endo had worked at the embassy for ten years, but he had resigned, as fate would have it, the night before the club party. He was therefore *not* an embassy employee at the time of his unfortunate demise.

No, the embassy did not find anything unusual or remarkable about his resignation.

Yes, it was certain no one had any idea why Endo was present at the American Club dinner-dance on the previous evening.

No, Endo had no security clearance. (The assistant shifted slightly in his chair.) Endo, it was amplified, was merely assigned to guarding the outside entrances to the compound on a rotating basis.

Yes, the ambassador would certainly be pleased to assist further in any additional inquiries.

The interview over, Kawamura was expressing gratitude for cooperation when he was surprised by the stolid lady, who approached and asked that her notes of the meeting be "approved." While the charges d'affaires stood and made polite conversation with the interpreter about his efforts to teach Russian at Tokyo University, Kawamura looked at the lady's notes. To his complete astonishment, the notes were taken in Japanese kanji—better than his own mother could write. Without pondering the ramifications of a police detective agreeing to notes taken by a representative of a potential witness to a crime, Kawamura signed his name to the bottom of the woman's notepad and hoped that the action would never come to the attention of Chief Arai.

"Well, what did you make of all that?" Kawamura asked the interpreter, who had still not uttered one word of Russian. The two men were walking along the winding driveway to the front gate of the embassy. They had been escorted to the building's entrance by the complete entourage minus the stolid lady.

"Amazing," answered the interpreter, nodding to the Japanese guard at the gate. "Absolutely amazing."

"I know," agreed Kawamura. "Absolutely amazing. They all sound like they were born in Tokyo."

★ ★ ★ ★

CHAPTER 21

"We should make Takeshita-san the murderer."

The speaker was the sergeant who had found the valves that drained the club pool, thereby flooding the neighborhood at the bottom of the hill. He was seated with Captain Kawamura and Police Chief Arai in the latter's office. His priority interest was, namely, to guide the discussion away from his own specific heroics in the affair—a topic of some ten minutes heated debate—toward the more general subject of the overall investigation.

"We'll make him confess, and then we won't have a problem dealing with all those foreigners," the sergeant added.

"Wait a minute," said Kawamura, "the facts . . ."

"Forget the facts," bellowed Chief Arai, interrupting. "What if we can't make him confess? Then we'll have even more problems." The veins in the Chief's temples were visible. "Use your head, sergeant, or you'll be back directing traffic."

Chief Arai was not having a good day. One murder on his turf was bad enough, even if it were a foreigner. The second murder, involving a Japanese who was, or had been until recently, working for the Russian Embassy, attracted all kinds of unwanted attention. And now that the early evening papers were out, Chief Arai found himself in the national spotlight.

Of particular interest to one and all was the whereabouts of the second body. Kawamura had reported that his team of investigators "had looked in all the logical places," but Pete Peterson's torso had not turned up. It would be only a matter of time before the Metropolitan Police Department would invade Chief Arai's little corner of Tokyo for the purposes of "administrative liaison and technical support." It probably would have happened already were it not a weekend. The investigation would then be taken out of his hands—a situation never good for one's career. Chief Arai turned his attention to Kawamura.

"Well, what *do* you have to show for your investigations? At least you got both heads."

"Yes, both heads," said Kawamura. "And I admit to being bothered by the fact that Mrs. Takeshita found the security guard's head in her bucket, and we found the bloody knife in her husband's locker. But there are two problems. First, the lockers are never locked. It's the custom there. Anybody could have put the knife in the locker."

"Where are the lockers?"

"On the same floor as the kitchen," answered Kawamura. "Across the elevator hall from the room where the head was found."

"That's the room with blood on the wall?"

"Yes sir, but . . ."

"Then there's no problem. Your idiot sergeant here is right," said Chief Arai, standing and leaning forward with his arms on the desk. "Just because anybody *could* have put the knife in the locker doesn't prove that Takeshita-san did *not* do it."

"That's why I said we should make Takeshita-san confess," added the sergeant from deep in the dog house.

"But," continued Kawamura, ignoring his sergeant, "the second problem is connected to the first one."

"What's that?" asked Chief Arai. The veins in his temples were pulsating visibly.

"According to our medical experts, the security guard, whose head was found in the bucket, was not killed by that knife. *His* murder was committed by the cleaver."

"The what?"

"The cleaver," Kawamura answered, making a chopping motion with his hand. "And the cleaver was found one floor below in the frozen-food locker. Not only that, Takeshita-san was not even on duty last night."

Chief Arai stared at his captain. For a moment, Kawamura thought the man's eyeballs would burst from their sockets and into his out basket.

"It was Mr. Peterson," Kawamura continued, "who was killed with the knife, and we don't know *where* that happened."

Chief Arai slowly sat down. His focus did not leave Kawamura.

"Captain," he said.

"Yes sir?"

"Tell your idiot sergeant to get out of here. And," he continued as the sergeant rose to leave, "tell him that effective Monday he's assigned to patrolling the street in front of the love hotel."

"Yes sir. Ah, sergeant, will you, ah, well, you know, ah . . ." commanded Kawamura crisply.

"I understand. It will be my humble pleasure," said the sergeant closing the door after him.

"Look Kawamura-san," said Chief Arai after a moment of silence during which he pounded the back of his neck with the brass handle of a ceremonial dagger presented on the occasion of his thirtieth anniversary with the force. "We've been friends a long time."

"Ah, yes sir."

"Try to keep calm and tell me exactly what you think."

"Well, in the first place, it's logical—at least at this stage—to assume that the security guard was murdered in the little room where his head was found. It's easier to carry a weapon away from the scene of a crime than a head."

"I don't think logic has anything to do with what happened in that madhouse," observed Chief Arai, "but go ahead."

"And I think the security guard's body was dumped into a laundry cart and brought up to the first floor using the elevator."

"Wait a minute," said Chief Arai. Before he continued he pounded the back of his neck several more times. "Why a laundry cart and, more importantly, why not include the head with the body?"

"The laundry cart was handy. Those carts are all over that building on almost every floor. There were two or three, for example, along the corridor leading to the elevator."

"What about the head?"

"I don't know," answered Kawamura simply. "Maybe the killer . . . Well no, he wouldn't have fogotten it, maybe he just . . . I don't know."

"So somewhere along the line, missing a head for his corpse, the killer picked up the general manager's head—which just happened to be lying around and put that in the cart." Chief Arai's veins were beginning to show again. "And then he took the elevator up to ground level and dumped the lot in the pool?"

"Well, put that way, it doesn't sound . . ."

"Another thing," said Chief Arai, standing and walking around his desk so as to lean over

Kawamura. "What was the security guard doing in the club in the first place?"

"There is something funny about that. He resigned from the embassy the day before, but according to his wife he didn't even come home that night. He'd been missing for over twenty-four hours when he was found in the pool."

For a second or two Kawamura was afraid the chief would explode. But the man managed to contain himself by taking a deep breath and then reaching for the dagger on his desk for some more furious pounding of the neck. He returned to his chair and sat quietly, studying the palm of one hand.

"I do have some theories," Kawamura continued, "that I should, hopefully, be able to prove or disprove tomorrow . . ." Kawamura stopped suddenly when he realized the chief had sliced the palm of his hand with the dagger.

"Are you OK, sir?"

"Wait a minute," said the chief, ignoring the question but still staring at his hand. "Can't you determine by blood type who was killed where?"

"No sir," answered Kawamura.

"Why not?"

"Because both victims were O positive."

"Oh," said the chief, throwing the dagger into the wastebasket.

★ ★ ★ ★

CHAPTER

22

Mrs. Takeshita and her husband rarely communicated. In the first place, Mrs. Takeshita's work hours—7:00 a.m. to 3:00 p.m.—precluded any conversation in the morning. She was long gone by the time her husband roused himself. Similarly, Mrs. Takeshita was more often than not in bed asleep by the time her husband managed to return at night. The job of purchasing for the club required being entertained, often until the wee hours, by a wide range of suppliers and prospective provisioners. The burden was awesome, but Takeshita suffered the responsibility admirably.

Mrs. Takeshita and her husband had another and more fundamental reason for seldom talking to each other. For years Mrs. Takeshita had supported the household through her earnings at the club. Managing a squadron of cleaning ladies, even if the management meant working along with others on the mop-and-bucket brigade, was nevertheless a departmental responsibility. Planning, preparation, and execution were as crucial to success as they were in any corporate empire.

Through the years Mrs. Takeshita's husband had been content to allow her to generate the family income base while he explored a number of promotional schemes designed to quickly swell the coffers. All his ventures, however, "bottomed out" sooner and deeper than anticipated, and it wasn't until he landed the job at the American Club, through Mrs. Takeshita's intercession, that his contribution to the kitty became anywhere near regular and steady. That was nine years ago. In less than a decade, due to several retirements and one unexpected death, Mr. Takeshita had made the startling jump from purchasing clerk to purchasing manager. And now he wanted his wife to abandon her career.

"It's beneath my dignity," Mr. Takeshita would tell his wife, the cleaning lady.

"But where was your dignity all those years before?" Mrs. Takeshita would respond to her husband, the purchasing manager. "Besides," she'd add, "we'll need my job when you get caught."

"Getting caught" was a possibility and a sore point between them. Mrs. Takeshita's concern about the potential problems resulting from accepting gifts and favors from suppliers was more a practical than moral question, and it invariably led to I'm-not-speaking-to-you-anymore resolutions that became easier to keep as time went by. They continued to sleep under the same roof, albeit at slightly different times, and that became the only common thread in their relationship. Mrs. Takeshita continued to commute to the club by subway while her husband drove a new Toyota to work and parked for thirty-six hundred yen a day at the Tokyo Tower. If by chance they passed in the club they ignored each other.

"The knife was found in your locker," Mrs. Takeshita stated the night after the club dance.

"And I wonder who put it there," he rejoined sourly.

*　　*　　*　　*

J.B. and Bumpy Culhane, on the other hand, communicated extensively with each other.

"Bumps, I must attend a reception at the Okura Hotel right after work. I'll send the driver to pick you up for the party later at the embassy and we'll meet there."

"How thoughtful of you Jack, but please try not to be late. We're nightcapping afterwards with the Women's Group president and thirty of her close friends."

"Splendid. How are the kids, by the way?"

"Who?"

"Our children."

"Oh. The maid will fix dinner and help them with their homework."

"Splendid," J.B. would say.

On the Saturday night after the American Club dance, J.B. and his wife found they had a rare and quiet evening to spend alone together. The scheduled party at the general manager's apartment, it goes without saying, had been canceled.

"This terrible thing at the club has the whole community upset. People are going ga-ga over it," Bumpy observed as the couple settled in for pre-dinner cocktails. "The rumor is that Pete was killed by the Japanese security guard from the Russian Embassy."

"Who then committed suicide by cutting off his own head?"

"Well, no," agreed Bumpy, "but *that* could have been done by an outsider who wandered onto club property. We all hope so."

"I'm afraid it's more complicated than that," said J.B. "Captain Kawamura—who seems like a decent fellow—thinks the two murders were committed by someone familiar with the inside workings of the club. Awareness of the procedures for bringing food to the top floor, knowledge of when the elevator corridor would be empty, and access to the, er, murder weapons all rule out a stranger."

"But that means it must be one of the employees."

"Or one of the members," said J.B., pouring another drink for himself.

* * * *

"You look exhausted," Tim Kawamura's wife stated as he flopped down at the low table in the center of their living-dining-bedroom. The two children had been given the other two rooms in the apartment for privacy while preparing, respectively, for high school and college entrance examinations. Western rock music rumbled from both rooms. Communication between Kawamura and his wife was inevitable, determined by proximity.

"It's more difficult than I thought to think and talk in both Japanese and English for hours at a time."

"What's it like at the American Club?" Mrs. Kawamura asked.

"It's a big place, many VIP members, and everyone seems anxious to help. Mr. Culhane, the president, said he'd invite us to dinner there after the crime is solved."

"Do you think you can solve the crime?"

" I will do my best to find out how it was done," said Kawamura to his wife. "And I have to prove who did it, and find one more body."

"Shouldn't you go to sleep now?"

"Probably. I'm due back there at 7:30 in the morning, and I still know nothing."

"Shall I lay out the futons?"

"Lay out the futons," said an exhausted Tim Kawamura.

* * * *

And in the western suburbs of Tokyo, communication between the club chef and his wife was uncharacteristically brief.

"Where is the sausage?" Yasuko cheerfully asked her husband.

"Where is the sausage? I have been interrogated, arrested, dragged to the police station, questioned again, released, dragged back to the club, questioned again, told to organize the staff for the normal Sunday brunch tomorrow, and you ask where is the sausage?"

"Yes."

"I'll get to it tomorrow. That is, unless I *really* chop off somebody's head," replied the chef.

* * * *

In the apartment rented by the club for the recreation director— a ten-minute walk down the hill past the Russian Embassy—Butch Percy and his wife got down to basic issues. It was something they both had avoided for over a year.

"You will have to tell everyone now, Peter," said Butch's wife.

"Don't call me Peter!" said Butch. "I hate the name, and I've told you a thousand times not to call me that. In addition, there is no reason to tell anyone anything, particularly now."

"But what about your job?" Mrs. Percy asked. "Can you, can we, continue to stay here?"

"Of course we can stay here. They'll need me more than ever now. I know more about this club than anyone—including the president."

"But don't you feel bad about what happened, about all of this?"

"Not in the least," replied the recreation director, pouring himself another Super Dry beer.

★ ★ ★ ★

CHAPTER

23

The telephone purred softly on the small table next to Gordy Sparks' side of the bed. This occurred at least twice a week, and invariably preceded crisp and chirpy remarks from communicators on the other end of the line wondering what time it was in Tokyo and whether Sparks was up and around yet. ("I'm always up and around at 3:00 a.m.," was all he ever managed to reply. Clever put-downs tended to fall woodenly on the uncomprehending

ears of folks ringing up in the sunshine of bright
Montana head office mornings.)

By mutual consent, the routine in the Sparks
household was for Mrs. Sparks to ignore these noc-
turnal intrusions and for Gordy to leap from bed and
stumble to the kitchen to handle the communication.
A pen and notepad were always positioned next to
the sink for the purpose of confirming details—
Gordy had once, in the fog of sleepiness, agreed to
accepting a shipment of seven thousand *tons* of beef.
An examination of hard data in the cold light of day
had fortunately allowed Gordy to change the operative unit to *pounds*.

"We have to meet right away," said the voice at
the other end of the line. *"Now,"* the voice added for
emphasis.

"What happened last night?" Gordy blurted out,
instantly regretting the sound made by his voice in
the darkened apartment. "You screwed things up,"
he whispered to compensate.

"I did not screw up. *You* were the one who wanted
to move the body," replied the voice.

"But what happened to Pete?" Gordy asked, again
letting his voice rise too high for the middle of the
night. "Pete had nothing to . . ."

"Stop talking," said the voice, "and meet me right
now."

"Where?" asked Gordy, squinting to read the 3:15
on the kitchen stove clock.

"Across from the love hotel is a snack bar. I'm
there now."

"You're in the neighborhood? You idiot, we shouldn't be seen together. We should . . ."

"Come immediately," said the voice. "I have an alibi for Friday night—you don't." The remark was immediately followed by a dial tone.

Gordy tiptoed back to the bedroom and stood silently watching the sleeping form of his wife bundled under the covers. "I agreed to this because of you," he thought to himself, "and now it's turned into a nightmare."

Fighting the urge to be sick—his stomach muscles tightened with the beginnings of the familiar spasms—Gordy went to the bathroom adjoining the master bedroom. An old pair of khaki trousers hung on the hook behind the door. Slipping these on over his pajama bottoms, Gordy stood for a moment in the darkness listening to his wife's breathing. She was sound asleep, but rummaging around in his closet for more clothes would be too risky.

Instead, he carefully left the bedroom area and felt his way along the walls and furniture to the front hall closet. He put on a pair of loafers and slipped his old leather jacket with the sheepskin lining over his bare shoulders. He remembered at the last minute to take the keys to the building from the wooden bowl next to the front door. He also remembered to take his umbrella. Outside—and these things can't be helped—it was a dark and stormy night.

The snack bar is an integral part of life in Japan. Serving neighborhood "regulars" primarily, snack bars provide for those otherwise cooped up in one-room inner-city abodes a loose framework for expanded social intercourse. Cluttered with magazines, newspapers, and adult comic books, snack bars offer warmth, conversation, the shared experience of TV viewing, the ready availability of food, plus the service of wine and spirits belonging to the regulars but kept on the premises. Licensing laws as a rule do not apply to the hours of operation—the more basic law of supply and demand dictates the extent of the business day. And with a love hotel offering twenty-four-hour tryst facilities across the narrow street, this particular snack bar remained open until the salarymen and office ladies caught the first morning trains back to the grind.

Gordy, together with a considerable amount of blowing rain, entered the establishment through the sliding door and were automatically greeted by the proprietress, a lady whose best years obviously coincided with those of the Occupation. Heavily rouged, rigidly lipsticked, and surprisingly bosomed, she looked up at Gordy from the comic book she had been examining. "Oh, welcome to our place, honey," she said in English.

Gordy pointed to the man huddled at the back of the room and squeezed his way past a couple seated at a low video-game table. Judging by their demeanor—the man was lightly dozing and the woman was worriedly fixing her hair—the couple had already availed themselves of the hotel facilities.

"You stupid bastard," Gordy hissed as he reached the rear of the room. "You really *are* crazy."

"Sit down."

"I'll sit down," said Gordy sitting down, "but I want an explanation of what happened Friday night."

"*You* want an explanation? I wasn't within twenty kilometers of the club the night of the dance." Conversation stopped as coffee orders were placed with the proprietress. "*You're* the one who was there," continued the speaker after the lady left, "and *you're* the one who wanted to . . . adjust . . . the evidence."

"Then what happened?" Gordy asked after taking a drink of water. The spasms were beginning again. "I didn't agree to this whole thing in the first place, and now . . ."

"You didn't agree? You certainly agreed when I said I'd take care of the problem. It wasn't my meat going in and out of the place."

"Yes, but . . ." Gordy stopped as the lady returned and served the coffee. She smelled of lilacs, he noticed, and the aroma mixed unfavorably with that of the coffee. He looked around the establishment for the entrance to the toilet, just in case.

"Yes, but," Gordy managed to continue after a moment, "I didn't think you'd go so far. And then the swimming pool thing . . ."

"I wasn't even there."

"Then who, I mean Pete . . . and his head . . . who did . . . the other thing?"

"That's what *I* would like to know."

The cockroach chose that moment to emerge from underneath the container holding the napkins and scurry in the direction of Gordy's coffee cup. It paused briefly and appeared to look at Gordy before ducking for the protection afforded by the lip of the saucer.

Purchasing manager Takeshita of the Tokyo American Club watched Gordy Sparks almost make it to the toilet door.

★ ★ ★ ★

CHAPTER

24

"Why did you not like Mr. Peterson?" Kawamura asked J.B. The two men were once again seated in the late general manager's office, which had become the "command center" during the investigation of the murders. It was Sunday morning and the full weekend food-service staff was on the scene preparing for the regular buffet brunch and dinner offerings. Facilities were being opened on a limited basis for the first time since the discovery of the heinous crimes of the previous Friday.

"Er, what?" replied J.B.

"We have the evidence, both from my men's study of the records and our interview with your club treasurer, that you wanted Mr. Peterson to be gone."

"Beans McCounter told you that?"

"Be . . . , ah, Mr. McCounter told us that you wanted to hire a headhunter to get rid of Mr. Peterson."

"Wait a minute . . ."

"And," continued Captain Kawamura, "we saw your letter in Mr. Peterson's file. It said he was on probation and contract cannot be yet renewed."

"Yes, but . . ."

"Kind of serious evidence, don't you think? A *head-hunter!*"

"You don't understand . . ."

"Decapitated in the pool."

"I know, but the *reason* for all that was . . ."

"And," interrupted Captain Kawamura again, "you told Be . . . , ah, Mr. McCounter you would make final decision this weekend."

"I know, but . . ."

"Final decision was kind of made this weekend, don't you think?"

"Hold it right there, Tim," J.B. said, abruptly standing and tipping over the wastebasket at his feet. "Let's get a few things straight."

Captain Kawamura, straight-backed in the general manager's chair, and J.B. Culhane, on his hands and knees picking up trash, were interrupted by the entrance of a waiter from the club coffee shop.

"I'll have a Bloody Mary instead," said J.B. as the waiter played around with cups, saucers, sugar bowls, and cream pitchers. "Double," he added.

"Now then," J.B. continued after the waiter had left the room. "What you don't understand is that Pete, er, Mr. Peterson, is, er, was, approaching retirement age. I didn't know his work well enough to be able to evaluate him. I didn't know how long he should . . ."

"So you wanted his head hunted?" interrupted the good captain.

"Not *his* head, someone else's head. I mean someone else's head *and* body—connected—to replace him. That is, in case . . ."

"So you did not renew his contract?"

"I only told him, in writing, that I wanted to delay any decisions until I got to know things better. That's businesslike. I've only been the president of this place for a couple weeks."

"Two months," corrected Kawamura.

"Seems like two years," observed J.B. "By the way, Tim," he added, sitting down and knocking over the wastebasket again, "is this the way you normally interrogate people?"

"I am not, as you say, interrogating. I am only asking why you hated Mr. Peterson."

"*I did not hate Mr. Peterson,*" J.B. was in the process of yelling from his hands and knees on the floor as the waiter arrived with the Bloody Mary. "Take this damn thing with you" he told the terrified waiter, handing him the wastebasket. "And bring another drink. And knock before you come in here."

"Don't loosen the cool," Kawamura counseled after the waiter left.

"I'm not loosening . . . er, I'm all right. Look, Tim, I didn't hate Mr Peterson. I just had to have options available in case he did retire and . . ."

"What is your retirement age at this club?" asked Kawamura.

"Er, I don't know, but . . . er, I don't think we have one for managers."

"Kind of thin excuse, don't you think? If you wanted him gone? And no real retirement age? And you get a headhunter?"

"I didn't get one. I just asked Beans how much those people charge for their, er, work. I just . . ."

"OK, I understand," said Kawamura suddenly rising and walking to the window. "You are innocent."

"Well, thanks a lot."

"Be . . . ah, Mr. McCounter said you didn't know anything."

"What does that mean, I didn't know anything?" asked J.B., also walking to the window. "I've only been president here for . . ."

"You didn't know about the internal audit. About the club's bad finances. About the problem."

"Wait a minute. What problem?"

"Because," Kawamura continued, "you are too new for the details."

"What is the problem?" J.B. found himself shouting as the waiter entered the room with another drink. He was balancing a service tray with one hand and knocking on the open door with the other. *"I didn't want to get rid of Pete because of a problem. I don't even know . . ."*

Kawamura and J.B. watched the waiter place the second drink next to the untouched first one. Without looking up, the waiter backed out the door and closed it.

". . . what the hell you're talking about."

"Don't be too exciting, J.B.-san. The audit shows that your club is ordering and paying for more beef than it is serving. The chef's records—he is a Spanish, by the way—and the purchasing records don't match. Many million of yen is the difference. And it could be that Mr. Peterson was involved."

"Pete," said J.B., "was never even *in* the kitchen. He knew many things about this club, but it's my understanding he never went near the food side of the business."

"Could be," replied Kawamura cryptically, "but maybe couldn't be. We are investigating that point."

"Well, I'm going to talk to my friend McCounter," said J.B. "I don't like being kept in the dark about things. If you need me further, Tim, I'll be with Beans or at home."

J.B. left the manager's office, stopped briefly in the men's room immediately adjacent to the "command center," then strode briskly toward the club's front doors. Early arrivals for the brunch were trickling in and the lobby was beginning to fill with members in their Sunday best. As J.B. reached the glass doors he heard his name called softly from behind. The coffee shop waiter trotted up and made his remarks apologetically.

"Don't worry, Mr. Culhane," said the waiter. "We also hated Mr. Peterson. All of us," he added.

J.B. walked out the doors and to his car in the club parking lot. Someone had backed into it, leaving a dent the size of a breadbasket in the driver's door.

★ ★ ★ ★

CHAPTER

25

Chef Juan Carlos was miserable. "Too much," he told himself. "This is all too much."

The murder of the club general manager and the discovery of his body in the swimming pool was obscene. "I will never swim in that pool again," vowed the chef, a man who had never swum in the pool at all.

The subsequent discovery that only the manager's head was in the pool and that the body itself belonged to a security guard from the Russian Embassy was the work of the devil. "Mon Dios," pleaded the chef, "forgive me for ever working here."

The finding of the security guard's head in a bucket next to the kitchen service area was for Juan Carlos an unspeakable horror. "From now on, I'm cleaning my own kitchen," the chef proclaimed to all who'd listen.

The general suspicion the police seemed to have was that because his knife and cleaver were somehow involved in the murder the chef was also involved. That was a grosspersonal insult. "I would *poison* my enemy with a tasty souffle," the chef thought, indignant.

And now to have strangers—worst of all policeman strangers—watching his every move in the kitchen was enough to tax the equanimity of the most callous of souls. Chef Juan Carlos was miserable.

Admittedly, preparing food for the Sunday buffet-style brunch was considerably easier than the more complex job of responding to random food orders from the menu. Most items could be prepared well in advance. Nevertheless, the Sunday staff in the kitchen was usually composed of rookies who required greater supervision, and to have strangers around and in the way was intolerable. Chef Juan Carlos thought momentarily of complaining to the manager, but then it was the manager's inconsiderate act of being murdered that brought about all the problems in the first place. "Why did I ever leave Barcelona," Juan Carlos lamented for at least the seventy-third time that weekend.

The sausage-making equipment was kept in a room that had originally been a corridor between the kitchen meat coolers and the baking ovens. The new refrigeration units were larger than the ones installed when the kitchen was built, and their bulk effectively closed off one end of the corridor. By contriving to have pantry shelves constructed at the other end of the corridor, Juan Carlos had fashioned a private workroom for himself, complete with a small gas range and refrigerator. It was there that he developed and tested new recipes, prepared special dishes, and made his sausage. The room was a haven away from the steam, heat, noise, and ordered chaos of the main food-service area.

Chef Juan Carlos told the policemen on duty in the kitchen that he had work to do and that he would be spending an hour or so in his private work area. "You don't follow me there for any damn reason," he said. One of the policemen did appear to express a genuine interest in how sausage was made, and after several minutes of agitated conversation, Juan Carlos relented. "You must help me then," he insisted. The policeman, a young man in his twenties, readily agreed.

The chef explained to the man that he regularly saved the fatty edges of meat that were cut off before being served to customers. He also showed the man how the judicious use of gristle and bone provided "body" in the texture of the product, and explained that this was particularly important in modern times since the use of hooves and other exotic parts of the animals was generally no longer possible. "Many good parts," Juan Carlos stated, "are thrown away nowadays."

The young policeman mentioned to the chef that his parents would probably have heart attacks if they saw him with his sleeves rolled up helping with the preparation of sausage. Eating meat of any kind was still an exotic experience to many members of the older generation in Japan, and in all cases the actual preparation techniques were never even imagined. "Traditionally," the young policeman explained, "only outcasts handled the flesh of four-legged animals."

Juan Carlos and the policeman discussed in a desultory fashion the details as they knew them of the murder mystery at the club. Helping Juan Carlos carry an open barrel of meat scraps from the cooler to the little room, the policeman admitted that he knew almost nothing, other than the fact that one headless body was still missing and that his buddies on the force were still searching the main building for it.

Showing the policeman how to calculate a proper balance of pork and beef for this particular recipe, Juan Carlos admitted that he had been lax in keeping control of the knives and cleavers in his armory. "They're all over the damn place," he stated, "and because of that I'm the first one to be blamed for the murder."

After stripping the meat from sundry bones—beef from bones as large as human thighs and pork from bones as relatively delicate as human ribs—Juan Carlos demonstrated how the introduction of ice to the mixture as the meat was being ground kept the fat from becoming too warm and separating into a gelatinous goo. "Ice," said the chef, "insures that the fat remains evenly distributed." Feeling suddenly like his grandfather, Juan Carlos revealed that "this is one of the secrets of good sausage."

"Slowly, young man, slowly," said Juan Carlos as the young policeman turned the handle of the grinder. They were the exact words, though not in Spanish, of course, that his grandfather had used so many years ago.

The chef was explaining that sausage casing was no longer made of the viscera of animals ("Many good parts of the animals are thrown away nowadays"), but was manufactured protein product both edible and infinitely preferable to the plastic product employed by American mass producers, when the young policeman's partner from the main kitchen entered the little room. Captain Kawamura, it would appear, had called a special meeting upstairs for all men on duty, and the young policeman's presence was requested.

Juan Carlos had also been explaining about "special relationships" in the club. He had mentioned to the young policeman that no one knew that he and Pete Peterson's wife were cousins. He was also about to mention another "special relationship" within the club that no one knew about—one that was perhaps more pertinent to the matter at hand—when they were interrupted.

Chef Juan Carlos shrugged his shoulders and wheeled the cart of uncooked sausage out to the ovens in the main kitchen. This, he thought to himself, will be a particularly good batch.

★ ★ ★ ★

CHAPTER

26

Captain Tim Kawamura watched his men dutifully walking through several theoretical reenactments of the crime. In one sense it would have been better if the reenactments had been staged the day before, when the club was still closed. But in another sense there was now a more realistic atmosphere provided by a working kitchen and service staff on the scene, creating their own noise, hustle, and confusion in and around the rooms and corridors as they went about their duties.

Essentially, it was determined that at least one of the murders had been committed in the little room next to the elevators at the B-1 kitchen level of the main building. Blood had been splattered on the wall of the little room and the security guard's head had been found in the cleaning ladies' bucket tucked under serving trays in the corner.

Across the corridor from the little room, a corridor that ran from the kitchen proper to the service elevator, was the employees' locker room and toilet. It was in one of the lockers that a bloody carving knife had been found. It was puzzling that the wounds on the guard's neck were not consistent with those that would have been administered by a knife, but nevertheless action of some kind probably took place within the general area.

The second area of interest for Captain Kawamura and his men was one floor below at the food delivery and storage level. It was here that the large meat freezers and coolers were located, and it was here, in one of the freezers, that a bloody cleaver had been found. Wounds from that instrument *would* have been consistent with the mayhem visited upon the security guard, but his head was found upstairs. "Knives, cleavers, heads, and bodies all in the wrong places," mused Kawamura to one of his sergeants, "and there is absolutely no logical reason for it." Could all of this have been some kind of terrible accident?" he wondered to himself.

On the ground floor next to the snack bar that serviced the pool area, Kawamura watched his men pretending to dump a head and body from a laundry cart into the pool. The investigators had carefully timed the speed of the elevator between the B-2 storage level, the B-1 kitchen level, and the ground-floor pool level. Theoretically, one of the murders could have been committed at the lower level, the second murder at the next level, and the dumping of body parts at the ground floor—all within forty-five seconds. In what order, why, and how remained the operative questions.

Kawamura turned his back on the charade he had created and squatted at the edge of the pool. He had given J.B. Culhane permission to refill the pool, and fresh water was being pumped from spigots at each of the four corners. Trailing his hand in the flow of water from one corner of the shallow end, Kawamura was surprised at how warm the water seemed to be. Then he remembered that J.B. had mentioned that the club had installed new heaters in the filtration system so that the facility could be used year-round.

The conditions today on the kitchen level, Kawamura realized, with waiters entering and leaving through the main kitchen doors to attend to the buffet, were similar to those between 7:30 and 8:00 on the night of the dinner-dance. No one on the staff had occasion to use the elevator between the time the food was delivered to the fourth floor and the dirty plates were collected and brought back to the kitchen area. Waiters were waiters, and they remained at their posts. Today it was the main dining room, last Friday it was the fourth floor. Cooks were cooks, and they always remained in the kitchen area. The four busboys assigned to relaying food carts up and down that night had no reason to hang around the elevator after the food was served; they took advantage of the break in the action to smoke cigarettes with the dishwashers at the opposite end of the kitchen area.

There was noise in the elevator corridor, to be sure, and there were always the quick trips by employees to the toilets in the locker room. The interesting thing, Kawamura realized, was that although the corridor would probably be deserted during the time at least one of the murders was committed, that fact couldn't be counted on. Whoever committed the crime had been very, very lucky. No one saw him, but then again he could have had anywhere from forty-five seconds to ten minutes to do the deed without accidental discovery. It all depended on luck.

This means, thought Kawamura, standing up and rubbing his knees, that it was probably a crime of passion. Only a fool would plan a crime which depended on a high degree of luck to escape detection. It had to be a spur-of-the-moment action—something resulting from a sharp word, a sudden accusation, an enormous misunderstanding, or a festering hate that time and circumstance caused to erupt.

Captain Kawamura excused his men from further variations on the reenactment theme and sent them back to their surveillance posts. He walked along the edge of the pool back to the "command center" in the former general manager's office. It was a lovely winter day, the sky was clear, the sun was shining, and on any other Sunday afternoon he would be strolling with his family in one of Tokyo's many parks and recreation areas. He would even, he thought, be able to converse with his daughter, who had become something of a recluse lately.

The 2:00 appointment was with Takeshita, the club's purchasing manager. For someone like that, someone about to be caught for carefully and methodically fiddling with the books to accommodate a gradual but large-scale theft from the club, sudden passion was not characteristic. He would have planned ahead and worked out the angles. Something was still wrong. And where, by the way, was the rest of Pete?

★ ★ ★ ★

CHAPTER

27

One of the things people working in the leisure industry learn early in their careers is that "weekend" means something else to them than to the populace at large. Butch Percy, American Club recreation director, had been on duty nearly every Saturday and Sunday of his adult life. That's when the real work is done. Days of rest were usually rainy Tuesday afternoons and Thursdays.

Butch's responsibilities at the club included the supervision of fifty or sixty employees—lifeguards, snack shop and bowling-alley employees, clerks in the videotape library, exercise center staff, front desk personnel, and random numbers of part-timers keeping things picked up and in order. Additionally, the painstakingly arranged "off premises" activities planned during weekdays actually took place on the weekends. Little League baseball games, family picnics, junior soccer matches, even golf tournaments required the recreation director's involvement if for no other reason than to help sort out last minute hitches in the scheduling. ("Hey, Percy, we're out at the baseball diamond and there are nine Japanese teams already here waiting to play. I'm putting an irate stranger on the phone, and I want you to straighten it out.")

But on the Saturday and Sunday after the Friday-night murders were discovered at the club, Butch had the rare experience of lolling about unoccupied with the bulk of humanity. He had been called to the club for questioning on Saturday afternoon, and had walked some of the police on duty through the recreation building on a cursory inspection tour of the facilities, but no one seemed to be seriously interested in his arena of activity. The recreation operation was shut down, and only the food service in the main building across the pool was open on Sunday.

Butch spent most of Sunday afternoon in a thoroughly exhausting manner—walking with his wife through the semi-fashionable shopping area of Harajuku. He had visited the neighborhood before, of course, but those trips were on rainy Tuesday afternoons or Thursdays. Crowds then were just crowds, not hordes. Today people were walking nine and ten abreast along the relatively broad sidewalks, and forward progress was a constant exercise in dodging, bumping, and slipping through cracks in the throng.

Waiting for his wife on the steps outside the Oriental Bazaar, into which she had ducked to check out lampstands or some such foolishness, Butch thought for an instant that he saw Angie Peterson, Pete's brand-new widow, walking along the opposite sidewalk. He had already noticed a number of familiar foreigners, and his mind must have been set to spot people he knew, because a second look determined that the girl across the street looked nothing like Angie.

It's funny, he thought to himself, Angie's attraction seemed to disappear with Pete's death. It was definitely exciting planning and executing their sessions together—Angie was a passionate and athletic lover—but he'd be glad when she cleared out. With Pete finally gone from his life, Butch wanted no one and nothing around to remind him of the man.

It *was* J.B. Culhane and his ever-friendly wife Bumpy *inside* the Oriental Bazaar, however. Butch entered the establishment to find out why it was taking his wife such an ungodly amount of time to look at lampstands, and there he found her deeply involved in a conversation with the Culhanes. The three of them stopped to stare at Butch as he wended his way toward them around the antiques and through the crowd of shoppers to the back of the store. As soon as he arrived, however, the conversation began again, with J.B. babbling something about visiting the club treasurer earlier in the day, Bumpy saying that the whole community was "gaga" about things, and his wife describing the innate beauty of an old Chinese urn she held in her hands.

"Well, we're just out walking around on my rare free Sunday," was Butch's contribution to a discussion that seemed to be going in three different directions. "It sure is crowded," he added.

Comments and observations slowly returned to the nasty business at the club, and J.B. was prompted to remark that he was gradually formulating the idea of a memorial service for Pete.

"Naturally, Butch," said J.B. in his best avuncular tone, "we would be, er, pleased if you could, er, prepare a few words—of your own choice, of course—for the, er, ceremony. But," J.B. added quickly, "it's entirely up to you."

Butch felt the delicate little bowl he had picked up from the counter crack in his hands. He looked up, but only Bumpy Culhane had seen it, and she turned her head away quickly.

"If it's all the same with you, sir, I'd rather not make any speeches," said Butch, carefully replacing the bowl on the counter. "I will attend whatever you plan, though."

"Well, er, keep it in mind," said J.B. "And if you change your mind, just let me know."

The two couples stood around for several more minutes admiring the Chinese urn, and then J.B. announced suddenly that he had some business to attend to. The Culhanes walked with the Percys to the cashier's counter, and while Butch's wife fumbled in her purse for her credit card, J.B. reached out and shook Butch's hand firmly.

"If you want to talk, son, call me anytime," said J.B. before he turned and walked toward the door. Bumpy lingered for a moment, touched Butch's arm, and looked him squarely in the eyes. She was about to say something, but instead turned abruptly and followed her husband out the door.

"What the hell was that all about?" Butch asked his wife. The Oriental Bazaar clerk, accustomed to a variety of languages and expressions, looked up briefly from his chore of wrapping the Chinese urn.

"I'll explain when we get home, dear."

"You'll tell me *now*," demanded Butch, causing not only the clerk to look up again but the lady behind the Percys to take a step or two back. Heated discussions between foreign husbands and wives at the cashier's station were not uncommon at the Oriental Bazaar.

"Please, Butch, you're making a scene. I think that . . ."

"I don't care what you think. *What were you and the Culhanes talking about?*"

The babble of shopping conversation in the crowded store virtually ceased. People shifted silently and surreptitiously for better views of the combatants. Group embarrassment and private intrigue mingled with the expectation of horror and excitement. The clerk, helpful in his misunderstanding, held up the partially wrapped Chinese urn with one hand on the top and the other on the bottom. Hands, vulgarly clasping the sides, would interfere with the appreciation of the urn's lines.

"*What?*" shouted Butch, removing all doubt that the issue was serious.

"I told the Culhanes the truth about you and Pete."

Most folks have at one time or another in their lives witnessed spontaneous and dramatic eruptions in the otherwise mundane conduct of societal affairs. The suddenness and speed of events makes interpretation difficult after the fact—angles of sight, position at occurrence and awareness of circumstances immediately preceding the action distort perception. Eyewitnesses are not as reliable as one would think.

Accounts differed as to whether the big foreigner actually pushed his female companion onto the counter containing beautifully displayed *imari* bowls and vases, or whether she slipped and destroyed the delicate merchandise in an attempt to avoid wildly swinging arms. Some thought the big foreigner deliberately shoved over the rack of plates and saucers in his mad rush to the door, others believed the damage was done by bystanders scrambling to avoid contact as he charged past. Even the collision at the doorway with entering customers happened too quickly to accurately judge. A middle-aged lady and two elderly men apologized to the fleeing form from their new position on the floor.

One detail was recalled with unvarying consistency, however. Everyone agreed that the clerk seemed to stand for a very long time, at least under the circumstances, with his hands grasping the top and bottom of what had once been an old Chinese urn—the big foreigner having destroyed its body with one swift blow to its midsection.

★ ★ ★ ★

CHAPTER

28

Why is it everyone asks me how I'm doing? Angie Peterson wondered to herself for at least the tenth time that weekend. There isn't an answer to that kind of question two days after a husband's death. And I'm not doing very well, she realized as she sat in her kitchen and began to cry again.

Angie's Sunday had been spent receiving concerned and well-intentioned members of the club community, mostly the wives of people who had worked in some capacity with her late husband Pete. Mrs. Culhane, the wife of the president, had spent over an hour with Angie explaining that the whole community was "ga-ga" over Pete's "unfortunate accident" and that her husband had promised to "get to the bottom of it all." Mrs. Sparks visited Angie and explained at great length how upset her own husband was over the matter. ("He got up in the middle of the night, walked around the neighborhood, and threw up all over himself.") Even that nice Mrs. Takeshita, the head cleaning lady, came in on her day off to offer help and support. The only wife Angie was glad she didn't see was Butch's wife; however, she at least called and the two ladies cried together over the telephone.

One pleasant surprise, Angie realized as she left the kitchen table and walked into the living room of the apartment, was the visit from the police detective in charge of things, Captain Kawamura. He delivered Japanese rice crackers and sticky donuts containing adzuki bean paste as gifts from his wife. He sat quietly while Angie served tea and ate two of the donuts. He said very little about Pete, but he seemed genuinely interested in Angie's friends and her immediate plans.

Because he seemed to listen so well—maybe it was a difficulty with the language—Angie found herself talking about her life and her frustrations as wife of the general manager of the club. He didn't even appear to judge her admission of a secret love affair as most people would do. He merely said it was a "natural human thing." He also mentioned, although it was completely unnecessary, that he was arranging for a policeman to be stationed outside the door of her apartment in case he could be of any help to her. Nice man.

Juan Carlos, working as the chef at the club, also paid a visit. Angie's father had been born in Spain but emigrated to the United States on his twentieth birthday. Angie had never met anyone from her father's side of the family until Juan Carlos showed up one day in Pennsylvania on the eve of her first marriage. It turned out that Angie's and Juan Carlos' fathers were brothers, and Juan Carlos, three years younger than Angie and something of an embarrassment, was, therefore, Angie's cousin. He had been on his way to an apprentice's job at a hotel in Hawaii when he stopped in on his "American family." Despite protestations and tears, Juan Carlos was invited to the wedding and proceeded to humiliate Angie by kissing her husband—the softball player from Scranton, Pa.— full on the lips. Worse yet, he bawled like a baby when Angie left the reception at the V.F.W. hall to embark on her honeymoon in Atlantic City. For as long as Angie was married to her first husband, his buddies gave him a hard time about that kiss.

"Well, Angela," said Juan Carlos as he entered the apartment, "it looks like you go back to the bank in Philadelphia." Juan Carlos had never fully approved of his cousin's second marriage to Pete.

"I don't need advice from you right now," replied Angie. "I just need some time to think things out, to make my plans slowly and carefully." Angie and Juan Carlos' relationship had settled to a level that allowed direct and often blunt remarks to pass between them without acrimony.

"But you should get out of here as soon as possible, Angela. You don't have any real friends here."

"I know that."

Juan Carlos walked over to the chair next to the telescope, sat down, and began to fine-tune the focus on the love hotel.

"Angela, who do you think it was that killed Pete?" the chef asked, still keeping his eye glued to the instrument. "I think it must be someone we both know."

"Probably," agreed Angie. "But for some reason I don't really care. Knowing who did it won't bring him back."

"For a while, the police thought I did it," said Juan Carlos.

"Did you?"

"Of course not, Angela. Pete never came in the kitchen. He left me alone."

Juan Carlos, looking through the telescope, and Angie, nibbling on a rice cracker, sat for several minutes in silence.

"That telescope might have something to do with Pete's death," Angie said at last.

"What?" asked Juan Carlos, turning to face his cousin.

"That telescope might have something . . ."

"I heard what you said, but what do you mean, the telescope?"

"Pete thought he saw him in the hotel with one of the girls from the accounting department. At least, he thinks he recognized the suspenders."

"What are you talking about, Angela?"

"The suspenders were those bright-colored ones. He saw them before they shut the windows, or drapes, or whatever they are."

"Who?"

And I think Pete threatened to tell everybody. They were arguing about Pete's employment contract."

"Who, Angela, who?" said Juan Carlos walking over and standing in front of the couch.

"Culhane."

"Mon Dios," said Juan Carlos, sitting down on the couch. "Mon Dios."

"But," added Angie, rising and walking toward the kitchen, "Pete told me he could have been wrong."

"Wait Angela, don't fix anything for me."

"Not even a cup of coffee?"

"Nothing. I have to get home. I only wanted to bring you this." Juan Carlos walking to the kitchen and placing the package on the table. "I just made a fresh batch of sausage, and you should eat some to keep up your strength."

Angie accompanied Juan Carlos to the door of the apartment and watched her cousin put on his shoe. For reasons that made sense only to Juan Carlos, he had taken off only one shoe upon entering.

"Culhane?" was Juan Carlos' last word as he went out the door.

"Culhane" was Angie's last word as she shut the door.

★ ★ ★ ★

CHAPTER

29

There were at least fifteen minutes before the meeting with Takeshita, and Captain Kawamura used this period of relative calm to reflect on his investigation to date. Seated behind the desk formerly occupied by Pete Peterson, Kawamura felt the eerie sensation that so often overcame him whenever he was alone with the personal effects of a victim of sudden death. Pete's desk was strewn with partially complete memos, cryptic notes to himself, an overflowing in basket, and a pile of neatly typed letters awaiting his signature. A half-smoked cigar, which Kawamura knew his staff had already "dusted" for fingerprints was back in the ashtray ready for its owner.

An examination of the photographs scattered around the room—some in frames, some propped against the wall on piles of menus and various club documents, and some in snapshot form organized in separate little groups—indicated that if nothing else Pete was gregarious. Pete often seemed to be having more fun in the photographs than anyone else was. And he seemed to have aged well. Early photographs showed him to be slender and straight, with a healthy mane of dark hair. The dates of the photographs could easily be determined by hairstyles— Pete went through a crew-cut stage as a young man, the hair became longer as it got grayer, and then there was the long sideburn stage which to Kawamura's way of thinking made him look slightly sinister—but in all cases the face and eye-focus remained firm and determined. Even the most recent photographs, one in particular with J.B. Culhane at what must have been his inauguration as president of the club, showed Pete as completely in control of himself and his surroundings. His hair by this time was snow-white.

Tim Kawamura made a mental note to himself, for at least the one hundredth time in his years on the police force, to make sure his own private affairs and papers were in order—just in case—and pulled his attention away from the immediate surroundings and directed it toward the summary he had compiled of the investigation to this point. Sudden death was an awful thing.

J.B. Culhane was probably not involved, at least not involved in Pete's murder. Witnesses placed him at the head of the table at all times during the dinner, and it was during this time that Pete was killed somewhere downstairs. Culhane also seemed genuinely ignorant of, among other things, anything going on beyond the lobby-reception area of the club operation. He would probably be as surprised that there were *not* Russian security guards prowling around the premises as he was when one was found headless in the swimming pool. He had exercised bad judgment in one respect, Kawamura recognized, in thinking that a "secret affair" of moderate intensity could be kept a secret among Japanese employed in the same organization. Twenty-seven of the club staff members found it necessary to report on the president's dalliance with someone named Midori in the accounting department. But that situation, plus a general uncertainty about Pete's performance, could not be developed into a scenario satisfying the motive, means, and opportunity formula. Culhane, as mysteriously accomplished as he was shallow, was not a suspect.

Kawamura looked at the next name on the list. Angie Peterson reminded him of the girlfriend of one of the Olympic javelin throwers he was assigned to protect so many years ago. A man, Kawamura thought fleetingly, might go to great lengths to become intimate with someone like that. Maybe golden hair was not as attractive to foreigners as it was to him, but a general consensus of all males of any kind would probably rank Mrs. Peterson fairly high on the universal scale. The problem, from Kawamura's point of view, was that she also could not have committed Pete's murder. She had never left the ballroom. But she could have been the magnet attracting a motive. Kawamura penciled an arrow from her name to that of Butch Percy.

Percy had not been a very cooperative interviewee, but his reluctance to reveal anything about his relationships within the club community could be traced to his affair with Mrs. Peterson. She had told Kawamura that the man was harmless, but he would nevertheless benefit—assuming he was willing to toss out his wife—by the death of his lover's husband. He was a suspect for sure, but Kawamura drew a question mark after his name. The security guard connection was still a mystery.

Chef Juan Carlos, at first glance, would be the perfect murderer. He was a volatile individual with access to all the murder weapons, had a barely tolerant relationship with Pete, and a knowledge of all that went on in the building's lower levels. He would also probably know about security guards on the

— 111 —

premises. But the obviousness of his behavior and attitude—he more than once threatened to kill Pete if he ever stepped into his kitchen—deflated the balloon of motive. Perhaps, Kawamura thought to himself as he drew another question mark, the good chef should undergo another interview.

Gordy Sparks was himself a question mark. Kawamura occasionally came across suspects as nervous and jumpy, and almost invariably they were guilty. But Sparks was nervous and jumpy about life itself. He was as upset by the questions about seeing the body in the pool from the fourth floor window as he was about the details of his job. His stated admiration of Pete and his denial of knowing the security guard were as blatantly frank as his statement of his own name. Sparks bore watching, but Kawamura wasn't sure why.

There were other possible suspects, of course, and Kawamura understood with depressing clarity that they could number in the hundreds. According to the statements taken by his men in the ballroom, over fifty people had visited the restrooms during the period in which Pete was killed. There were also the late arrivals who could have run into Pete on their way into the club. A connection between those guests and the security guard would be difficult to imagine, but that connection was just as difficult to make with the employees. Large as the organization was, there had to be hidden passions relating Pete, the security guard, and someone—member, employee, or outsider—wandering onto the premises.

Captain Kawamura dropped his pencil on the desk, closed his eyes, and leaned back in Pete's chair. It was a more comfortable chair than the one in his office. At times like this, when the pressure increased with each new roadblock in the course of an investigation, Kawamura's thoughts turned to the cool, clear lakes in his native area of southern Japan. To be walking along those shores, or, better yet, seated in a rowboat with a fishing pole, was as close to paradise as anything he could imagine. Concentrating on a float in the water, to the exclusion of all other earthly concerns, was purifying.

Kawamura had almost purified himself to sleep—after all, it was now Sunday afternoon and he had barely six hours' sleep since he was called to the American Club on Friday evening—when a knock on the office door brought him back to shore. One of his sergeants delivered the club purchasing manager, Takeshita, for his 2:00 appointment. Kawamura took one look at the man and immediately decided the tack of his questioning. And asking hard questions was going to be a whole lot easier in Japanese.

★ ★ ★ ★

CHAPTER

30

Gordy Sparks saw it all. From his living room window in Azabu Towers, overlooking the American Club grounds, he saw Captain Kawamura walking Takeshita around the pool area. The two men were being followed closely in their stroll

— 113 —

by what appeared to be a very solidly built policeman dressed in the gray "action uniform" favored by the riot patrols and criminal-arrest officers.

Captain Kawamura and Takeshita were deep in conversation. If anything, it appeared that the club purchasing manager was doing most of the talking. Many words were going back and forth and, judging by gestures perceived from a height of ten stories, the discussion was at times somewhat intense. The policeman in the gray uniform remained at all times only a step or two behind Takeshita.

Gordy realized the game was over when the two men, plus the gray policeman, entered the rear door of the main club building next to the pool snack-bar area. Takeshita hesitated for a moment and pointed up in the direction of Gordy's apartment before he was firmly pushed through the door and out of sight. Gordy instinctively stepped back from the window when Takeshita pointed, but then realized it didn't make a difference anymore.

The sliding door in the living room of the Sparks' apartment opened onto a ledge that ran around the perimeter of the apartment. The ledge was actually the roof of the building proper—Gordy's penthouse had been constructed as a separate entity on top—and it served more as a space for plants and outdoor potted trees than as a normal balcony. Gordy had only been on the ledge once before—the day he and his wife rented the apartment.

Gordy slid the door shut and stepped carefully to

the railing at the edge. He had originally been terrified of heights. In fact, the tallest building he had ever seen until he left for college in Boston was the three-story department store he used to visit with his grandmother when he was a young boy. There is not much need to build things high on the plains of Montana.

Mastering little fears and phobias was something Gordy had struggled with most of his life. He wrestled uncomfortably with public-speaking courses in college, fear of heights when he took his first job in a midtown Manhattan tower, and the terror of commitment when to his surprise he found himself engaged to be married.

Dogged determination more than psychological adjustments got Gordy through the difficult times, however. Even accepting his present job—representing in Japan the Western Association of Meat Producers—brought challenges that had to be conquered through sheer force of will and unwavering stubbornness.

Taken on an inspection trip of a slaughterhouse near his old hometown in Montana, the holder of a prestigious masters degree in marketing and economics had to be helped from the sawdusted earth where his faint had landed both him and his Brooks Brothers suit. Gordy did have to smile, though, as he recalled the good-natured teasing he'd endured from his new employers. ("Hey cowboy, you have a special attachment to that beast?")

Shadows cast by the recreation building in the setting sun extended across most of the pool area now. It begins to get dark during Japanese winters before 5:00 p.m. Gordy found himself focusing on the very edge of the shadow as it crept across the rippling water.

Of all the colossal mistakes in his life, joining forces with Takeshita was by far and away the greatest. The impact was made worse by the realization that it was a liaison born of weakness—*his* weakness.

The Association was about to terminate his employment contract unless sudden and dramatic improvements developed in "the Japanese sector." Gordy had been hired to unclog, if possible, existing meat-distribution channels in Japan and to develop new and more effective channels. The main idea was to establish a position that could be exploited as the restrictions on importing American beef were gradually eased. A secondary condition, of course, was that during the unclogging and developing-new-channels phase, sales had to improve. Businessmen, not statesmen, were paying his salary.

To be honest about things, there were conflicting interests on the American exporting side. U.S. grain producers, for example, made more money on their sales to Japan than the U.S. beef producers could ever hope to make. Japanese cattle, providing Japanese beef, not only consumed American grain, they were also responsible for a profitable sub-industry involving the exportation of American alfalfa cubes providing "roughage" for the animals. Dried rice stalks wouldn't do the trick.

The resulting balance-of-trade battles between conflicting interests within the U.S. created irregular and uneven pressures on the Japanese government. And these, perceived as weaknesses by the Japanese side, meant barriers would last to the bitter end. His job was not as easy, Gordy knew, as everyone seemed to think.

The deal whereby Takeshita would purchase huge quantities of U.S. beef for the club and then resell the product out the back door was only a short-term solution to Gordy's problems, to be sure, but at least it raised his sales three to four percent above the budgeted increase curve. It was a mere blip on the graph, but it could be pointed to as an indication of positive change. And positive change meant another quarter in Japan with a job.

Gordy had not been interested in local profits from this venture with Takeshita, and had merely believed the man's protestations that significant portions of the profits were used to take care of the chef anyway. Whatever Takeshita was doing, it seemed to be far enough away from Gordy so that the whole matter could be ignored. And then the awful revelation of murder cropped up.

The damn security guard from the Soviet Embassy had gotten wind of peculiar things happening in the club's supply area. One of his posts had been literally next to the supply entrance, and midnight deliveries *from* the club could in no way be considered normal. Takeshita had vowed to handle the guard's clumsy attempts to get in on the action by promising the guard that he'd be hired as a waiter, and from that inside position he would be able to share in the spoils. Gordy had agreed with Takeshita up to that point because it involved what Takeshita called a "normal Japanese solution" for circumstances in which knowledge was power. Somehow, Gordy had figured that the details would not concern him.

Gordy heard his name called; the sound of his wife's voice was barely audible from inside the apartment. He moved from his position immediately outside the door of the living room and walked to an area of the ledge opposite the solid wall between the living room and kitchen. His wife had been over visiting Angie Peterson, and he was not ready to listen to her talk about it.

The impact of Takeshita's revelation on Thursday night that he had taken care of the guard permanently was a horrendous physical shock, greater than anything Gordy had ever experienced in his life, at least up until that time. He had sat listening to Takeshita in the Highlander Bar at the Hotel Okura totally stunned. How could one human being kill another human being, and then sit quietly relating the details?

Takeshita had told the guard to show up at the club in a tuxedo for a "dress rehearsal" of the service routine to be choreographed for the gala annual dinner-dance to be held the following evening. Because he was to be a "non-regular" employee, the guard was instructed to enter the premises through the rusty service-entrance door. Not knowing any better, he did.

On the pretense of showing the guard the "service equipment," Takeshita had lured the man to a meat cooler where frozen beef was thawed for twenty-four hours before delivery upstairs to the main kitchen. It was at this stage of Takeshita's explanation that Gordy excused himself in order to be sick in the men's room outside the entrance to the Highlander Bar, but not, however, before Takeshita had described the act of hacking off the guard's head with a cleaver brought down from the kitchen for that very purpose.

In a trance—his mind numbed by shock—Gordy had discussed the pros and cons of what was to be done now that the awful deed was accomplished. Takeshita had maintained that the dismembered body was safe where it was. The club staff would be too busy upstairs during the Friday dinner-dance to go near the meat cooler, and the evidence, in the former person of Yoshio Endo, could be removed from the premises the following night along with the surplus beef destined for greater Tokyo's *shabu-shabu* and *teppanyaki* parlors. "The body," Takeshita had said, "will keep in the cooler."

Gordy had argued that, on the other hand, a chance discovery of a dead body and accompanying head (Good God, could this be true?) in *any* area of the club remotely connected with beef was certain to bring about an investigation of all remotely related issues. Inflated sales would be revealed!

The meeting that night before the dinner-dance had ended unsatisfactorily. To Takeshita it was a question of some fifty-five to sixty million yen; to Gordy it was a question of keeping his job for another couple of months, or face public humiliation. Complicating the issue, Takeshita had revealed that he had not gotten around to "taking care of the chef."

Gordy's wife was turning on the lights inside the apartment. Shadows completely covered the pool area, and Gordy could see lights going on in the club lobby. It was not dark yet, but almost.

Gordy had made his mind up during the cocktail party preceding the dinner-dance. Downstairs, ticking like a time bomb, was a dead man, a stranger, a nonentity capable of bringing problems to a head before solution a to the problems could be formulated. Gordy had taken advantage of the general chaos between the time everyone had been seated and the time the soup was served to go down to the delivery level of the club to disperse the evidence—to separate the meat from the meat. To hell with that fool Takeshita.

It took several precious minutes to locate the security guard in his two parts. In retrospect, it was clear that a casual visitor to the cooler—a room not much larger than a typical master bedroom—would not immediately spot the victim. The head was in a cardboard box on a shelf slightly above eye-level. The body, tuxedo-clad, was stretched out behind rows of thawing hams and massive cuts of prime rib ready for the Sunday buffet. The cleaver was nowhere to be found; Takeshita had said something about throwing it into the main freezer next to the cooler.

Dumping the head into the laundry cart was not particularly a problem. The only thing Gordy had to touch was the cardboard box. The thump of the head onto the pile of dirty towels in the bottom of the cart almost sent him over the edge, however. He swallowed quickly and firmly to suppress the bile rising in his throat.

The body was a different matter. Gordy dragged it by the ankles from its resting place to the laundry cart. To regain his composure, Gordy walked to the door of the cooler and looked out over the crates of food supplies piled in the delivery area. He had gone too far to quit, or be sick, now. He returned to the body, and with one sweeping motion picked it up— making a point of not looking at the puckered neck barely emerging from the white shirt collar—and dumped it into the cart. The only sensation he allowed himself to register was the chill of the tuxedo fabric. The lack of discernible heat in the thing made the corpse seem less than human.

Gordy had no specific plan as to where the head and body should go. His only concern was satisfying the overwhelming desire to remove the evidence from his beef. Each centimeter of distance improved matters. If he could get everything up to the ground level, he would have options that included the recreation building, the club parking lot, even an over-the-wall exercise that would dump the problem on the neighbors below.

When the elevator stopped at the B-1 kitchen level, Gordon W. Sparks' heart almost stopped too.

★ ★ ★ ★

CHAPTER

31

The elevator doors opened on the corridor, now empty, leading to the kitchen. Gordy stood frozen, one hand over his mouth, the other on the corner of the laundry cart containing the remains of the security guard. The sound of pots and pans banging, mingled with the voices of kitchen personnel, echoed down the hallway. But, Gordy realized, he was still for the moment alone.

Laundry carts, identical to the one with him on the elevator, were lined up along the wall of the corridor. To the left was an open doorway through which Gordy could see a number of wheeled service trays. On the right, clothing lockers were visible through another doorway.

The automatic closing of the elevator doors surprised Gordy sufficiently to shock him back to reality. Something had to be done, and in a hurry. He jammed the palm of his hand against the elevator's OPEN button, pushed the laundry cart out of the elevator and into the little room on the left. No one had seen him. As he stood leaning with his arms on the cart and wondering what to do next, he heard the elevator doors shut. This was followed by the whine of gears and rotors which meant the elevator was on its way to another floor. And *that* meant it could be bringing back a visitor. In less than a minute!

Merely abandoning the cart was an option, but the little room was obviously a work station currently being used for the dinner service upstairs on the club's top floor. The contents of the cart would be discovered immediately—perhaps before Gordy could get back to the dinner. The same could be said of the problems that immediate discovery would bring if he just wheeled the cart into line with its brothers outside in the corridor. Gordy realized he was standing in center of a sudden, and very temporary, food service calm that was about to return to conditions of storm. The whine of the elevator stopped, and Gordy could hear the doors open somewhere up the shaft.

He grabbed the cleaning bucket and mop that stood in a corner of the room behind several obviously broken service trays. Using the mop handle to leverage the security guard's body at the shoulder, he reached into the laundry cart and removed Yoshio Endo's head by his hair. He dropped the head into the bucket, then carried the bucket back to the far corner of the room. He piled domed service-tray lids over the bucket, and pushed the broken trays back against the corner. The whining of the elevator started again.

Gordy was again standing and leaning with his arms against the cart, looking down at the other half of a problem requiring an immediate solution, when he realized that the pitch of the noise made by the elevator was changing. It was stopping. At his floor!

Leaving the cart where it was, Gordy dashed across the corridor and into what turned out to be an employees' locker room. He was certain that whoever was on the elevator hadn't seen him; the doors were just opening. But he did notice, out of the corner of his eye, that several of the cooks had been standing at the other end of the corridor in the entranceway to the kitchen. He couldn't be sure, but he thought— hoped and prayed, actually—that their backs had been to him.

Gordy found the toilet at the near end of the rows of lockers that seemed to stretch all the way back to the area near the kitchen entrance. As is the case with most facilities behind the scenes in Japan, the toilets were used by both sexes. Gordy walked into one of the stalls containing Western-style facilities, closed the lid on the toilet bowl, and sat down to gather his wits. Dear God, he thought, don't let a woman come in.

He could feel the familiar spasms beginning in his stomach, but for the first time in his life he realized he was too terrified even to be sick. Looking at his watch he realized that he had only been gone from the cocktail party upstairs for about ten minutes, but those had been ten of the most horrible minutes of his life. And the other half of Yoshio Endo must be disposed of in less time than already spent on the project.

Gordy left the stall and walked to the door. He opened it, and was about to enter the locker room proper when he saw a tuxedo-clad form swing around from the entrance and go off in the direction of the long rows of lockers. He couldn't be certain—it all happened so quickly, and the lockers blocked his view—but the form seemed to be strangely out of place.

That's it, said Gordy to himself, leave things where they are. It suddenly became obvious that the only thing to do was get back to the dinner before the security guard's body was discovered. Gordy tiptoed to the door of the locker room, aware of the sound that the new visitor was making by opening and shutting a metal door, and cautiously looked out into the corridor.

It was empty—the cooks at the far end had apparently gone back into the kitchen. The elevator doors were closed, and the indicator light above the doors showed that the elevator was at the B-1 level. It was too bad if they found the body in the laundry cart, but maybe the fact that it was headless would complicate things enough to throw everyone off the meat trail. The problem was, of course, that they'd find the head pretty quickly—it being in the same room and all.

Gordy took a deep breath, and made a dash for the elevator. He glanced into the little service room expecting to see the laundry cart where he had left it. The shock took his breath away. The cart was gone. But the headless body, as if taking a breather from the rigors of ballroom dancing, was seated on the floor against the wall.

Holy Christ. Now what?

Gordy grabbed the last cart lined up along the corridor, wheeled it into the little room, picked up the body, and dumped it into the cart. The only sensation Gordy registered was that the tuxedo fabric was no longer cold to the touch. Room temperature warmth had returned the torso to something seeming more human. And the torso was beginning to bleed. Gordy punched the elevator button and entered with the laundry cart. As the doors closed behind him, he heard someone running along the corridor trying to catch the elevator. As the gears and rotors began to whine, Gordy took his finger off the CLOSE button, and heard someone angrily slam what must have a fist against the B-1 doors. He made it to the ground level of the building, and in the seven seconds it took for the trip, he hit upon the perfect place for the torso. It had nothing to do with the swimming pool.

Now, standing on the ledge outside his penthouse apartment in the Azabu Towers complex overlooking the American Club, Gordon W. Sparks made up his mind. The humiliation of failing in his job was something that with time he would get over. It would not be easy for his wife—she had become accustomed to the expatriate life with the same energy she had displayed in resisting the move to Tokyo in the first place. She was inside the apartment now probably arranging place-settings for the Women's Group luncheon she was hosting tomorrow.

But the fact remained that Gordy was in too deep for the problems to just "go away." There would probably be a trial, and his name would become synonymous with panic under pressure, but eventually facts would emerge that would prove that, other than tampering with evidence, he was basically innocent. Careful scrutiny of his bank account and modest investment portfolio would confirm that he did not partake of whatever profits that Takeshita had realized from the re-sale scam.

It was dark now, and lights in the surrounding neighborhood were on. It was unusual to see the club recreation building in darkness, and all the floors above the dining room in the main building were equally dark. Presumably everything would be back to business-as-usual on Monday morning—that is, everything except affairs in the Sparks household.

Gordy heard the telephone inside the apartment ringing. His wife would answer it, and it wouldn't surprise Gordy if good Captain Kawamura was calling to ask if he could visit. The noose was already tightening.

Gordy had been loaning against the railing on the edge of the building for what must have been a very long time. The sun had still been in the sky at first, but now it was dark. It was when Gordy pushed with his hands against the railing to straighten himself that the support gave way. To be fair, the railing was never intended to be more than a decorative adjunct to the ledge outside the apartment.

For a moment, Gordy teetered on the edge of the ten-story building. He swung his arms backward trying to pull his center of gravity back from the abyss, but he realized he was moving forward. He held out as long as he could, but against all logic he stepped forward—into thin air. Mercifully, he was probably unconscious from the time he banged his head on his downstairs neighbor's balcony until he landed in the Azabu Towers parking lot—thirty-two feet per second per second away.

★ ★ ★ ★

CHAPTER 32 "That was Captain Kawamura," said J.B. Culhane to his wife Bumpy as he returned to the living room. It was early Sunday evening, the Filipina maid was sporting about in Roppongi on her day off, and the Culhane offspring were in their rooms pretending to do their homework. It was the one time each week that the family "roughed it" for the evening meal—they ordered pizza, yakitori, or Chinese food delivered. "He wants me to go over to the club immediately," continued J.B. "He said there are new developments."

"Oh pooh," said Bumpy Culhane with feeling. "You shouldn't have answered the telephone. I knew it would be something bad."

"Well, he said it was extremely urgent, so maybe he's solved the crime."

"I hope so. The whole community is . . ."

"I know," said J.B. "Ga-ga."

"That's what *I* was going to . . ."

"Look, Bumps," said J.B., cutting the conversation short, "Kawamura-san tried to insist that I wait for one of his squad cars to come here and pick me up. But I'll be damned if I'm going to be dependent on them all night. I'm taking my own car over there. Otherwise I might not get home until midnight, or whenever they're ready to bring me back. If one of those guys comes here, tell him I've already gone to the club."

"But what about dinner?"

"I'll get something there."

"I mean *us* here," Bumpy said.

"Oh, er, get one of the kids to order something. Better yet, try the sausage the chef dropped off. I understand it's very tasty." There are times . . ., J.B. thought to himself as he put on his Harris tweed sports jacket and went out the front door.

The garage in the basement of the Culhane residence was shared with the other tenants in the building, and maintained in a spotless condition unlike anything J.B. had ever experienced. For some reason—either the special construction of the automobiles or the behind-the-scenes scrubbing by elves and pixies—the normal grease and oil stains never seemed to accumulate in black puddles under the vehicles. He certainly hadn't been cleaning *his* parking space.

J.B. had a choice of two cars—the company car that was commandeered during the week by the driver, or his wife's little Honda with the brand-new dent in the door. The Honda was easier to handle, but because J.B. knew the driver disapproved of anyone else getting behind the wheel of the company car, J.B. chose the company car. Authority must be asserted every now and then.

It was probably his fumbling with a relatively unfamiliar set of keys that saved J.B.'s life.

The steel bar crashed down a microsecond after J.B. bent over to pick up the keys he had dropped on the floor. The follow-through of the bar, after making a deep indentation on the edge of the car's roof, shattered the door window, ripped a six-inch gash in the door itself, and thumped J.B. in the small of the back.

Once the shock of the sudden violence began to subside, the pain was excruciating. J.B. realized he was lying flat on his stomach, and his legs seemed disconnected from his body. He turned his head to look up in time to see the bar swinging down on him again. Someone was standing there trying to kill him.

J.B. jerked his head away and the bar hit the concrete floor inches from his cheek. He saw the sparks this created, and smelled the heat generated by the impact. A chip of concrete sliced the skin on his forehead.

In the brief moment it took for his assailant to raise the bar for another blow, J.B. scrambled under the car. He used his elbows primarily to propel himself; his feet felt numb.

The next blow, however, had the effect of demonstrating that he still had feeling in his lower extremities. Although apparently deflected by some part of the car—J.B. heard the bar crash against metal before it hit him on the back of his thigh—the pain was enough to cause him to raise his head suddenly and thereby bang it against the undercarriage of the car. In anger and in pain, J.B. screamed. The bar poked him once under the car, and then it stopped. He screamed again. And then there was nothing.

The babble of voices got closer. Could there be more than one of them? J.B. wondered. It seemed to have some effect before, so he screamed again. A moment or two passed, and then he almost cried with relief when he saw the uniform hats on the heads of the policemen peering with great curiosity under the car.

It took a while to sort things out. J.B. had difficulty standing up straight at first, but fortunately the blow to his back had missed his spinal column and instead struck the large muscle running parallel to it. It would be a long time, however, before he'd be able to take deep breaths comfortably, or get in and out of chairs without a struggle.

The injury to the hamstring in his thigh made it difficult to straighten his leg, and J.B. spent some time hobbling around in circles bent over from the waist. Combined with the sting from the cut on his forehead, the ache of a banged skull and, to his surprise, the newly apparent pain of an index finger missing a fingernail, J.B. felt as if he'd been thoroughly trounced in battle. Not only that, he realized his clothes had managed to soak up a surprising quantity of slippery, but clear, oil. (It's there, but you just don't see it in Japan, J.B. thought to himself.)

The car, of course, was a mess. In addition to everything else, the blow intended for J.B.'s leg had been dampened by the steel bar's contact with the lower part of the car's rear door. The gash extended from the door, down through the chrome trim, and into the panel beneath the door. It would almost be worth it to see the driver's reaction on Monday morning—even bird droppings tended to infuriate him.

The police had arrived in the nick of time—their chore had been to ferry J.B. back to the American Club. One of the policemen had already found the weapon. A wrecker's prising bar had been left on a pile of construction material near the garage's rear entrance. Fresh paint marks matching the color of the car were clearly in evidence on the bar. The assailant, interrupted in his mayhem by the sound of the police car entering the garage, had obviously thrown the weapon back onto the pile while making his escape.

After considerable conversational fits and starts—disjointed phrases, partial sentences, mysterious words, and some graphic sign language—the following points were made reasonably clear to all parties on the scene. First of all, Mrs. Culhane was not to be alarmed by hearing what happened. J.B. would tell her about the attack when he was ready. Next, J.B. would immediately accompany the policemen to the club. Something was said about a suicide and the fact that the crimes had been solved. Finally, and most important from J.B.'s point of view, the police could measure, photograph, fingerprint, and diagram the garage all night long for all he cared, but someone must be discreetly stationed outside his apartment door to guard against the attacker's possible return. It took awhile, but eventually everyone understood.

The ride to the club was something out of the movies. Red lights flashing, horns and sirens wailing, and a loud speaker system enabling the policemen to scare other drivers out of their wits with amplified commands to move the hell over, resulted in the normal ten-minute ride from J.B.'s residence to the club—albeit with looping lane changes and a brief spurt down the wrong side of a street—to be accomplished in just over nine minutes.

The scene at the club, as the car carrying J.B. screeched into the parking lot, was also like the movies—the making of movies. Bright spotlights shown down on the pool area, and "extras" in the form of members who had been dining at the evening buffet stood in the open space between the two club buildings, casting long shadows along the pool deck.

The brightest lights were focused on the Azabu Towers apartment building immediately behind the club. Tenants of the building filled most windows, and all seemed intent on the comings and goings of a dozen or more actors dressed up as policemen in the general area of the doorway between the apartment and the club property. J.B. was overwhelmed by the feeling of déjà vu—it had only been two nights since all of this happened before.

He had only a few moments to reflect on that thought as his companions from the police car insisted he be brought immediately to the "command center" in the former general manager's office. I do believe, said J.B. to himself as he limped across the parking lot and painfully crawled up the four steps to the club's entrance, that things are beginning to get out of control.

Captain Kawamura was behind the desk, which was cluttered with not only documents pertinent to his investigation but also with the remains of several *o-bento* meals. The two untouched Bloody Marys were in the same spot J.B. had left them earlier that day. Across from Kawamura was the club treasurer, Beans McCounter. Beans was sitting in one of the guest chairs with his hands on his knees, his mouth open, and his eyes focused on something several light-years away.

"Hello, Tim," said J.B. to Captain Kawamura. "And, er, hello, Beans."

J.B. carefully eased himself into the other chair, noticing all the while that McCounter hadn't moved a muscle—hadn't even blinked.

"Is he OK?" J.B. asked.

"Probably," Kawamura answered.

"What happened out there? I understand from one of your men that someone committed suicide."

"Yes, suicide," the captain confirmed. "And we think that closes the case."

"Who was it?"

"I'm afraid it's your friend," replied Kawamura. "Mr. Gordon W. Sparks."

"What?" said J.B., starting to stand, then changing his mind. He looked over at McCounter, but Beans hadn't even twitched. He was still staring straight ahead with his mouth open. "Gordy wouldn't hurt a fly, in fact he was probably afraid of flies. He couldn't . . ."

"He was not alone. Your Takeshita-san was involved. He even confessed to committing the first murder. We have Be . . . ah . . . Mr. McCounter to thank for catching them."

J.B. glanced at McCounter, then looked back at Kawamura. He took a deep breath, slowly reached forward and picked up one of the Bloody Marys. He offered it to Beans, but there was no reaction.

"Well, Tim," said J.B., deciding to drink the thing himself. "This may take awhile. You tell me your story first, then I'll tell you mine."

Captain Kawamura stared at J.B. for a moment, then looked down at his notes.

"I was afraid there was going to be more," he said.

★ ★ ★ ★

CHAPTER

33

According to Captain Kawamura, Takeshita, the club's purchasing manager, had been ordering greater quantities of beef than the club could possibly use. The amount had gradually increased each month over a period of a year. A surprisingly simple distortion of records, agreed upon by Sparks and Takeshita, kept this fact from coming to the attention of anyone at the club.

By using a wholesaler with a direct relationship with Sparks' sources, the cost per unit of beef could be easily controlled. A kilogram of a certain cut of meat may cost five thousand yen at the wholesale level, but by the time it goes through an extended distribution process, the cost to the end-purchaser could be five times that amount. By cutting out the middlemen—a risky proposition in Japan—nearly five times the amount of meat could go in and out of the club doors at the same overall cost. Unit costs were still recorded at the old numbers, but the real number of units was five times higher.

"Takeshita-san told us that Mr. Sparks agreed because the real damages were to the middlemen, not to the club," said Kawamura. "He was only interested in increasing volume. He didn't care what happened to the meat afterwards."

"But," said J.B. Culhane turning to the club treasurer, "even though the true volume wasn't known, there *were* increases. Don't we have some kind of system to confirm that our purchases match our sales?"

Beans McCounter continued to sit with his hands on his knees and his eyes focused on space. Without closing his mouth, he slowly shook his head back and forth.

"Are you sure he's OK?" asked J.B., looking back at Kawamura.

"Be . . . ah . . . Mr. McCounter told our investigators," continued Kawamura, ignoring the question, "it is difficult convincing your chef keeping accurate records is important."

"He is Spanish . . ." put in J.B.

"I know. And you said before 'like an artist,' " confirmed Kawamura.

"Yes," said J.B., rewrapping his handkerchief around his nailless index finger. "But what about the murders? Why do you think Gordy had anything to do with them?"

"This afternoon Takeshita-san confessed to killing the security guard from the Russian Embassy. He is not a very nice man, by the way, your Takeshita-san."

"Why?"

"Because he killed . . ."

"No, I mean *why* did he kill the guard?"

"He killed the guard because the guard found out that the meat was being shipped back out of the club for resale," said Kawamura.

"But why didn't Takeshita-san do something sensible? Like bribing the guard, for example?"

"He probably didn't do anything sensible because of size of money involved. Be . . . ah . . . Mr.

McCounter thinks it could be around sixty million yen that . . ."

"Holy smokes," said J.B., looking at the club treasurer. J.B. noted that Beans made his second movement in fifteen minutes—his Adam's apple bobbed, indicating a tight little swallow.

"And then he hid the guard's head and body in the meat cooler downstairs. That confused my investigators about time of death because meat cooler can preserve, ah, things in it, and then the warm water of the heated swimming pool, sort of. . ." Kawamura's explanation began to trail off.

"But how was Gordy involved?" asked J.B.

"Takeshita-san told us that Mr. Sparks was unhappy about leaving the, ah, body parts near the meat. Mr. Sparks went down to the cooler on the night of the dinner-dance and, ah, tried to redistribute everything."

"How do you know that?"

"Takeshita-san told us, and he has perfect alibi for night of dance."

Captain Kawamura explained his conclusion based upon Takeshita-san's report of the conversation he and Gordy Sparks had had in the snack bar across from the love hotel on the Saturday evening following the party. Gordy had apparently described to Takeshita the circumstances and condition of the evidence that only Takeshita could know. There was no reason for Takeshita to lie, or at least distort the content of the conversation, since he was already, albeit reluctantly, on record as having committed the first crime.

"And our investigators' conclusion is that the general manager, Mr. Peterson, surprised Mr. Sparks in moving the evidence around. In a panic, which you can imagine in the situation, Mr. Sparks killed Mr. Peterson."

"Where is Pete's body, then?"

"Takeshita-san doesn't know. Mr. Sparks did not admit to killing Mr. Peterson when he talked to Takeshita-san. We were on our way to arrest Mr. Sparks when he . . ."

"Committed suicide?"

"From the top of his building. Be . . . ah . . . Mr. McCounter," said Kawamura, nodding in the direction of the club treasurer, "was kind enough to identify the body in the building's parking lot. It landed," Kawamura amplified, looking down at his notes, "on a 1971 white Nissan Fairlady 240Z, which already needed to be washed."

Beans McCounter made his third movement of the meeting by nodding his head slowly.

"Are you happy with the solution, Tim?" J.B. asked after a moment's pause. He had a difficult time leaning forward to reach the second Bloody Mary glass. The alcohol helped ease the pain— in a way that was most probably not medically advised—but the stiffness was closing in like nightfall. "I mean, excluding the fact that Pete's body seems to have disappeared."

"It *could* have happened that way. And then suicide is, ah, the atonement of guilt." Kawamura looked down at his notes, out the window at the circus of flashing lights and movement, and over at Beans before looking back at J.B. "But I am not happy with the solution, J.B."

"Well, listen to this. We still have a mystery, Tim."

And with that, J.B. described his adventure in the garage of his apartment less than half an hour ago. Captain Kawamura interrupted the report only once to observe that he had wondered why J.B.'s clothes suddenly appeared to have gone decades without cleaning.

J.B. spent more time detailing the injuries to himself than he did detailing the ones to his car, but it became obvious to Kawamura that the affair was a whole lot more than mere violence for the purpose of scaring the victim. This was violence meant to kill. Even Beans turned his head and gazed in the general direction of J.B.

"It all happened so fast, I didn't have time to be as frightened about it then as I'm becoming now." J.B. looked at the bottom of his empty glass. "If I hadn't dropped my keys, the bar would have split my skull wide open."

"Do you think it has anything to do with the meat business?"

Beans' sudden question startled Kawamura. "I don't think so," he replied after a moment's thought.

J.B. just looked perplexed. "Everyone knows I'm too new in the job to know anything about it," he said, looking at McCounter. "I think it's something else. Some of the policemen are still looking for evidence. And Tim," he said, turning to Captain Kawamura, "I asked one of them to guard the door to my apartment. I don't want my family involved in whatever's going on."

"This is very serious, J.B.," said Kawamura, reaching for the telephone. "Did you see who it was?"

"I only saw the person from the knees down. He was wearing men's shoes."

"Is it possible he *thinks* you recognized him?"

"Well, that's possible, I guess."

Kawamura handed the telephone to J.B. "That could be just as bad. Call to your home right now."

★ ★ ★ ★

CHAPTER

34

In retrospect, it would have been better if J.B. Culhane had told Captain Kawamura about being attacked in his garage right away. Precious minutes had been spent discussing Takeshita's confession to the murder of the security guard and the subsequent suicide of Gordy Sparks.

Captain Kawamura, perhaps influenced by his youthful study of British mystery books, was quicker than J.B. to recognize the potential for disaster in the attacker's savage behavior.

Radio contact was made immediately with Kawamura's men inspecting the mess in the Culhane garage. Confirmation was obtained that the police guard was still in place outside J.B.'s apartment door. No one, according to the report, had entered or left the apartment since the guard's arrival.

J.B. was not able to reach anyone in his apartment by telephone, however. There was no answer, even though he tried the number three times. The significance of this—the realization that the attacker could have immediately gone to the Culhane apartment even before the guard took up his station—was nearly overwhelming.

Kawamura instructed his men to forget about the garage and to secure the area in and around the apartment itself. This meant, if conditions warranted, to break in with the expectation of violence.

Kawamura and J.B. went immediately from the general manager's office to one of the police patrol cars in the club parking lot. Beans McCounter trailed behind.

The scene in the parking lot was still one of considerable confusion. Club members, not really clear as to what was going on, stood around in small groups or tried to mingle with the policemen in attempts to gain some hard data on the situation. Two grisly murders had been committed on the premises Friday evening, and now there was another death, a Sunday suicide next door, that apparently was connected in some way.

It was from this chaos of spotlights, sirens, flashing red lights, and morbid curiosity that Captain Kawamura and J.B. departed at great speed for the Culhane residence. It was noted that the president, quite obviously hobbled, a cut on his forehead, and a bandage on one hand, was escorted to the police car by detectives at each elbow. The treasurer, seemingly in shock, watched the departure and then, ignoring all questions, wandered into the shadows and off into the black Azabu night. The rumors this sparked were spectacularly creative.

Kawamura again established contact with his men at the apartment as the police car left the club property and sped past the front gates of the Russian Embassy. Lights were burning in the apartment, sound from the television was audible, but no one answered the door. J.B. listened to the two-way communication—conducted professionally and with a minimum of words—with increasing dread. They were *his* loved ones not answering the door. In fact, it was quite possible that he hadn't even locked the door when he left for the club forty minutes earlier.

By the time the police car reached the major intersection at the corner, it was decided that the police should enter the apartment. J.B. listened to the dead air crackling over the radio, and then the terse remark, translated for his benefit by Kawamura, that the door was locked. "No," J.B. answered to the subsequent question, "there is no superintendent on the premises with a key."

The police car made the left turn at the corner of the intersection by literally forcing its way into the flow of traffic. J.B. heard the crunch of metal on metal as the car clipped a white delivery van that had pulled to the side a fraction of a second too late.

A shiny new BMW was nudged from the rear by the police car with sufficient force to cause it to jump the curbing and come to rest against the cement pillars supporting the overhead expressway. The fact that the police car didn't even slow down during this disruption of the orderly flow of things in Japan made the situation seem more terrifying to J.B. Captain Kawamura and his cohorts considered the affair to be very serious indeed.

By the time the police car reached the bottom of the hill and began a right turn, again forcing its way through traffic, communication on the radio revealed that the door to the apartment was too solid to break down with equipment immediately available. It was decided, Kawamura translated for J.B., to prepare an assault through one of the apartment windows. J.B. mentioned that the balcony door was usually left unlocked, and this initiated more conversation between Kawamura and his men on the spot. J.B.'s inquiry as to whether or not this presented special problems elicited no response from Kawamura. He was staring straight ahead as the car roared through the Juban and up the hill past the Austrian embassy.

J.B. knew his wife was not one of the braver souls on earth. Her concept of "adventure" was limited to events in which the parameters of control were well established and recognized by all participants. Bumpy preferred costume balls and organized tours to pub-crawling and rafting down the Colorado River. If the attacker were polite, she'd be inclined to invite him into the family room for buttered pop-corn and hot cocoa.

The two-way radio crackled to life as the car passed Nishimachi International School, attended by one of the Culhane children, imparting the infor-mation that movement was discerned inside the apartment by two officers who had gained access to the balcony of the apartment next to the Culhanes. Positive identification was impossible because the curtains were drawn. That would be the master bed-room, J.B. informed Kawamura.

This particular stretch of road was one lane in width, and an iron railing had been erected to protect people walking along the narrow sidewalk. Traffic was backed up by cars waiting for the light at the five-street intersection fifty meters ahead. Although the police car siren was blaring, the cars ahead of it, not certain of the direction from which the warning sound emanated, only gradually crept through the intersection to clear the way. It was the most frus-trating part of the trip, and it prompted J.B. to smash his fist down on the dashboard.

"Don't get exciting," soothed Kawamura. "There's not much we can do anyway."

J.B. vowed to resign as president of the club as the police car reached the intersection and turned right. The apartment was only a couple hundred meters away. Being president was not all that it was cracked up to be. The prestige was nice and it looked good on a resume, J.B. thought to himself. But assuming responsibility for everything on a voluntary basis was for masochists only. Why not just enjoy the club and let someone else do the work? And now all this tragedy.

The police car screeched to a halt at the front entrance of the apartment building. An Azabu Fire Department truck had just arrived and uniformed men were unloading a ladder that would presumably be used in gaining access to the Culhane apartment. Lights from the public tennis courts and baseball ground across the street illuminated the neighborhood. People walking dogs, playing ball, or just passing through the area stopped to watch the unfolding drama.

Captain Kawamura indicated to J.B. that he should follow him into the building and to the elevator leading to the third floor. Although charged by the adrenalin surging through his system, J.B. nevertheless found it difficult to keep up with the policeman. The leg was one matter—it was now becoming extremely difficult just to walk. But the injury to his back made it painful even to breathe. J.B. began to worry seriously about a heart attack as he clumped into the elevator behind Kawamura.

Officers had just broken through the front door to the apartment as Kawamura and J.B. reached the third floor. Standing to one side of the door, resembling Beans McCounter in his open-mouthed vacuity, was one very obviously traumatized pizza-delivery boy. He stood with the white pizza box balanced on the palm of his hand, and looked as if he hadn't moved for several hours.

J.B. entered the apartment behind the policemen, even though their gestures and motions indicated that he should wait in the hallway. He had to get to his family.

The lights in the living room were on but the television was playing to an empty room. J.B. heard muffled shouts from the hallway leading to the bedrooms. Most of the words were in Japanese, but one voice rang out with a "Leave me alone!" in perfectly clear English.

J.B. limped toward the hallway and made it as far as the door to the kitchen when another policeman charged past him, solidly knocking him against the wall. The man had been carrying a portable two-way radio and was shouting instructions into it as he ran down the hallway.

J.B. leaned against the wall for a moment trying to catch his breath. The thought that he might faint flashed through his mind. It was a terrible feeling being so helpless, but even if he were fit it would be impossible to get past the policemen gathered outside the master bedroom door.

A woman's scream—Bumpy's—startled everyone and produced about one second of silence. Then the policeman carrying the radio shouted the Japanese for "one, two, three," into the instrument. The crash of the bedroom door being slammed open was nearly simultaneous with the sound of a heavy plate-glass window being smashed. The fire department ladders had brought more police in through the bedroom window. There were sounds of a scuffle—grunting, a thump against the wall, and a slew of angry words—then nothing.

J.B. pushed his way into the room. The place was a shambles. Bedding was strewn about the floor, lamps and tables were knocked over, and the pictures—some of individual family members and others of close friends—lay trampled and broken.

Bumpy Culhane jumped up from the bare mattress and ran to her husband. Throwing her arms around his neck was enough to knock J.B. off balance, sending them both reeling backward. Fortunately, the corner of the splintered doorway helped break their fall.

"The kids?" asked J.B. in a voice choked with emotion, relief, and pain.

"Your children were locked in the bathroom," said Captain Kawamura. "And they seem OK."

The two children, relieved to be released from what must have been an hour of sheer terror, charged the embracing couple. It wasn't just two falls on his injured back in as many minutes that was solely responsible for J.B.'s temporary lapse of consciousness

It was also the raging glare of animal madness on the face of the intruder, now firmly in the clutches of two burly policemen. Pete Peterson, Jr.—living all those years with the name "Butch Percy,"—had clearly, and frighteningly, snapped.

★ ★ ★ ★

CHAPTER

35

Captain Kawamura allowed J.B. to stay behind at the apartment while the family arranged its affairs for the evening. A half dozen policemen also remained, absorbed in the task of measuring and cataloging the debris in the bedroom.

Bumpy had told Kawamura that Butch had seemed to be obsessed with a desire to destroy any evidence of family togetherness. Photographs and pictures were particularly appealing targets.

Butch had herded the family into the master bedroom for the obvious purpose of maintaining control and preventing the escape of any members, which might have been possible in the more open living area. It was apparently the only logical behavior exhibited by the man during the siege.

He had spent the entire time ranting and raving in the bedroom, smashing objects at random, and waiting for J.B.'s return so that he could "finally kill him." When the children slipped into the bathroom and locked the door, Butch yelled through the door that he wouldn't harm them—he merely wanted to kill their father. "Then you'll know," he had said.

"It was strange," Bumpy told Kawamura. "although he constantly screamed at me, he called me *Mrs.* Culhane the whole time, as if I were an impartial bystander, as if he wanted my approval."

J.B. had promised Kawamura that he'd join him at the Azabu Police Station when things settled down. Bumpy would be excused from making an official statement until the morning, but J.B.'s presence was essential for sorting out details. "Many forms have to be completed," Captain Kawamura had said.

Friendly neighbors in the building offered the Culhanes lodging for the night, and the offer was accepted with alacrity. Not only was the apartment, at least the master bedroom, a mess, it also appeared that investigators were planning to spend many long hours ensconced therein with their studies.

Additionally, the phone calls were beginning. A number of people, some of them virtual strangers, rang up on the flimsiest of pretexts and seemed to get around to the "what's new?" question after only brief opening formalities. One young man, an American working for *The Japan Times,* came right out and asked if it was true that J.B. had been arrested for the crimes at the club.

It was already after 11:00 p.m. when J.B. arrived at the police station. Kawamura and his men had elicited a confession of sorts from Butch. It had taken skillful questioning—there had been frequent lapses in rational response—but a picture of what had really happened at the club on Friday night slowly emerged.

Seated in Kawamura's office, sipping burnt black coffee which underlings kept producing from a machine somewhere in the building, J.B. and the good Captain compared notes and conclusions. J.B. was certain he felt worse than his companion, but he wasn't sure about who looked worse. Kawamura, tie loosened and shirt collar unbuttoned, dark circles under his eyes, an impressive stubble, and a unique tangle of hair, which now revealed more gray than was previously apparent in its neat, well-combed state, had the look of a man coming in from a long march of several days duration.

"I didn't know that Butch Percy was Pete Peterson's son," said Kawamura. The observation was not quite a challenge, but close.

"I only learned this afternoon that Pete was his father. We ran into, er, Butch with his wife while we were shopping. His wife told us. She knew that her husband wanted to keep the relationship a secret— something about avoiding charges of favoritism— but she was also worried that after his father's death, her husband had exhibited no natural signs of sadness."

"He told our investigators," said Kawamura, "he was 'fathered' by Pete when he and his mother worked at Palmer House Hotel in Chicago, but that marriage ended or something soon after he was born."

"I, er, had no reason to know that," said J.B. "I've only been president, for, er, not very long."

"And he said that he was adopted by a big shot in Chicago named Percy—a man who married his mother—but that marriage lasted only a couple years. I think he was not happy when he grew up."

"If Butch kept this a secret," said J.B., "do you think Pete knew about it?"

"My men don't think so. I know one thing though. Pete's wife Angie doesn't know."

"How do you know that?"

"Because Butch was having an affair with her."

"What?" J.B. exploded. He would have jumped from his chair if his body had permitted. "You're not serious. That's unthinkable!"

"It's true, though," said Kawamura. "She told me."

"That's terrible. There's a word for that kind of thing."

"The word," said Kawamura, making a face as he sipped from his coffee cup, "is revenge."

"Well, I see what you mean. That's something for the psychologists to puzzle out. But I still can't imagine it."

"Normal people have hard time to imagine many things," said Kawamura, rising from his chair. He walked to the door of his office, closed it, returned to his desk, opened the bottom drawer, and pulled out a bottle of Suntory Very Fine Old Whisky. Reaching across the desk, he filled J.B.'s cup, put the bottle back into the drawer without taking any for himself, went over and opened the door, then returned to his chair. "But we learned many things tonight," he continued. "And this mystery business is finished."

"I'm glad," said J.B., but would you kindly tell me what the hell happened?"

"Of course," agreed Kawamura, "My guess was right."

"I'm glad to hear that, too. But what happened Friday night?"

"In the first place," said Kawamura, "I always knew that Mr. Sparks could not murder anybody. He had no nerve."

"Well, I suppose that was a point in his favor."

"Yes, there were really two crimes committed that were completely unrelated."

"But what about Gordy's suicide? You said . . ."

"Wait a minute. One by one, please," Kawamura said, running his fingers through his hair. "In the first place, it was very easy for your Takeshita-san to kill the security guard from the Russian Embassy. He had stolen enough money to last him for years. Killing to protect that was not problem. Takeshita-san was not a nice man."

"I accept that," said J.B. "But what happened that night at the club? Gordy was moving the guard's body and, er, head around . . ."

"Yes, moving them around. But he was only trying to remove the evidence from any connection with meat. In a way, it was a coincidence that he was even in the kitchen area that night."

"What was it Gordy told Takeshita-san about, er, moving the evidence?" J.B. asked.

"He told Takeshita-san that he heard somebody coming on the elevator after he hid the head in the bucket. He then ran away and went into the toilet in the employees' locker room. After a few minutes, he went out. Whoever had been there, was gone. He also told Takeshita-san that someone took the body out of the laundry cart while Gordy was in the toilet and sat it up on the floor leaning against the wall."

"What on earth?"

"I know. It sounds strange," said Kawamura. "I thought when I heard the story that Mr. Sparks was in too much panic to think or remember things clearly. He told to Takeshita-san that he picked up the body and put it back into a cart and hid the body again also."

"Where?"

"He didn't tell that to Takeshita-san. And Takeshita-san didn't ask."

"But the whole thing is ridiculous," said J.B. "Why would anyone take a headless body out of a laundry cart?"

"No one did. That's the point. The body seated on the floor was the, ah, newly killed body of Pete. Without knowing it, *that's* the body Mr. Sparks hid."

"If that's the case, then what happened?"

"Butch told us tonight that he followed his father from the dinner-dance on the top floor down the elevator to the kitchen level."

"Why?"

"No one knows. Maybe Pete was checking the food."

"I mean," said J.B., "*why* did he follow Pete?"

"Because he wanted Pete to renew his work contract. Pete didn't want him here."

"How do you know that?" asked J.B.

"Because your treasurer, Be . . . ah . . . Mr. McCounter, said that Pete wanted to hire a headhunter to look for a new recreation director. He asked how much those people charge for their, ah, work."

Christ, thought J.B., images of small fish being swallowed by a string of progressively larger fish flashing in his head.

Captain Kawamura got up from his chair and closed the door. He repeated the process with the whiskey and J.B.'s cup, opened the door, and returned to his chair.

"I hope you can realize," said Kawamura, "that Butch is a little out of control, and his confession is not one hundred percent clear. He was obviously out of control that night."

"I can realize . . . er, I understand. What happened next?"

"Butch wanted to get the general manager to change his mind about the firing. Butch wanted to stay in Japan. They argued about it as they went down in the elevator. Apparently Pete was stubborn about it. It must have been them arriving at the kitchen level that Mr. Sparks heard."

"What happened then?"

J.B. shifted uncomfortably in his chair as he imagined the heat, steam, and noise in that part of the building.

"Well, from what we understand, Pete got off the elevator with Butch, still talking about keeping his job. Pete apparently saw that one of the laundry carts was not where it should be —was not lined up along the wall."

"That was Gordy's cart?"

"Probably. He began to move it back to where it should be, and Butch was standing behind him, talk-

— 155 —

ing. According to my men's information, we learned that Pete suddenly bent over and looked at something inside the cart."

"Oh, oh."

"Yes, oh, oh. I think at this point Butch had no clear idea about anything. A large carving knife was on one of the serving trays with some domed lids used by your people for roast beef."

"I know."

"Anyway, Butch picked it up. By the way, J.B., at this stage my men had difficult time to get Butch to talk about anything except the look of the back of your general manager's neck as he bent over the cart."

"That's revolting!"

"More revolting is that he announced that he was his son—then swung the knife down on the back of Pete's neck. Pete's head fell into the cart."

"That's the most terrible thing I've ever heard in my whole life," said J.B. struggling out of his chair.

"The body fell on the floor against the wall. Remember we saw those blood marks?"

"Oh my God," said J.B. sitting down again and drinking half of the cup's contents.

"Butch then went to the employees' locker room and hid the knife in the locker most far away from the door."

"Takeshita-san's locker."

"Takeshita-san's locker. He had seniority on the floor, and the best locker is the one that's most private. I don't think Butch knew whose it was."

"And it was during this time that Gordy left the toilet and went out and saw the body on the floor?"

"Yes," answered Kawamura. "Pete must have moved the original cart enough before he was killed so that Mr. Sparks thought it was gone."

Captain Kawamura repeated the routine with door, coffee cup, and whiskey bottle—this time looking at the bottle for a moment before replacing it in his drawer.

"Then," he continued, "Butch returned to the little room and got the cart to take it . . ."

"Wait a minute," interrupted J.B. "He left . . . er, his father's body on the floor. Gordy took that thinking it was the security guard's body and hid it. But didn't Butch think it was strange that a body was already in a cart with . . .er, Pete's head?"

"Hard to say. He makes love to his father's wife. He kills his father. What's strange to him? He said to my men he didn't care—didn't even wonder—how body got into the cart. He took everything upstairs in the elevator and dumped it all in the swimming pool. It was the perfect place to, ah, humiliate him, Butch said to us."

"Holy shit," said J.B., carefully leaning back in his chair and looking at the ceiling over Kawamura's head. The green paint was peeling. "Butch must be insane."

"Yes, certain," replied Kawamura simply. "Or at least crazy," he added.

"But where is the rest of Pete? That's as big a mystery as anything else."

"That," said the good captain, "is the only end still loose."

★ ★ ★ ★

CHAPTER

36

The sun was already dawning on a new day—and worst of all a Monday—when the Azabu Police Department car deposited J.B. Culhane at the front steps of his apartment building. It, to say the least, had been quite a weekend.

The gala Friday night dinner-dance had looked at first as if it would be a raging success. All the necessary elements had come together and the atmosphere had been one of very pleasant and relaxed elegance. It was not easy, J.B. reflected, organizing complex functions in a club with 3,500 families from forty-four countries. In addition to the large number of people, there were forty-four cultural standards and social expectations that also had to be taken into account. Sushi, popcorn, red wine, reggae music and the Mormon Tabernacle Choir were all fine things in themselves, but it was always necessary to draw lines so that the component parts complemented an organized whole. Only if the organized whole was sufficiently impressive would the popcorners and toe-tappers forget their individual causes.

Things had been going very well indeed until poor Gordy Sparks made his spectacular announcement about things being amiss in the pool. It must have been, J.B. thought to himself as he again fumbled with keys—this time trying to enter his apartment building—an overwhelming shock to Gordy when he saw body parts floating in the swimming pool. It had only been minutes before that Gordy, trying to protect his reputation, had scurried around in the bowels of the building hiding a head in a bucket and a body God-only-knows where. Then to come upstairs, try to compose oneself from the horror of the experience, and to see what he thought was safely out of sight bobbing lazily in the water, must have shaken him to the core. No wonder he threw up all over the place.

J.B. stepped into the elevator. A hard knot of pain had formed at the back of his left leg, and his back felt as if he was being gripped in a large vice. Pushing the elevator button with his damaged index finger, he concluded that this injury alone was sufficient reason to resign from the club presidency and to stay home from work. The loss of the nail would prevent him from signing his name. J.B. leaned his head against the elevator door while he waited for it to take him to his third-floor apartment.

The suddenly opening doors nearly sent him sprawling on his face, but he regained his balance as his bad leg slipped forward and caught him. Looking down, he saw he had stepped on a square white pizza box containing a complete pizza, unaccountably left on the floor outside the elevator. Christ, he thought, will this never end?

Gordy's behavior during the episode was in no way excusable—in an indirect way he really *was* stealing from the club—but his motives and actions were at least understandable. He had panicked, first about his job and then in trying to cover up the crime, but panic levels in individuals vary depending on a wide range of personal and professional pressures. Gordy Sparks just buckled a lot sooner than most. Kawamura had indicated that there was some preliminary evidence that the suicide was really an accident, but he couldn't be certain until the ledge outside the Sparks' apartment was examined during the daylight. J.B. couldn't imagine what the evidence would be. Do people leave notes stating that they are *not* committing suicide?

The situation with Butch Percy was different. Here was a man who had been obviously harboring great hatred for a father he never really knew until he ended up in Japan working for the man. And then to kill him in cold blood for real or imagined wrongs from forty years ago—without even confronting him about the relationship until a second or two before his death—was beyond all comprehension.

J.B. dropped his keys on the floor as he tried to enter the apartment. He flinched instinctively, and turned his head in a back-wrenching twist. He had nearly been killed the last time he dropped his keys, and he wondered if the reaction would be with him for the rest of his life.

Thinking back on what he could remember about Pete's résumé, he did vaguely recall that Pete had been married briefly while still a teenager in Chicago. He also seemed to recall, however, that Butch had worked at the club for almost a year before Pete was employed. *That* must have been a shock, learning that his hated father had been hired to be his boss.

It was a few moments before J.B. realized he was alone in the apartment. Of course, he remembered, the neighbor with the curly red hair—Beth something—had agreed to take the Culhane family for the night.

J.B. walked into the kitchen and checked the refrigerator. Bumpy never cooked, and tasty leftovers were rare and unexpected treats. Other than things for the children, the refrigerator offered slim pickings.

There *was* a magnificent-looking sausage from the chef, and J.B. took it out along with two eggs and laid them on the counter. It's funny about the chef, J.B. thought. The man had the type of volatile passion that could conceivably lead to the commission of all the crimes of the weekend. Yet he was always doing sensitive and thoughtful things. Captain Kawamura had even mentioned that the chef had arranged for one of his sausages to be delivered to the police station. He must basically be a nice man, J.B. concluded.

While the frying pan heated over the burner, J.B. went to the bedroom. His clothes were sodden with invisible grease and oil, and the muck seemed to have soaked through to his skin. A pink ribbon, obviously hung across the doorway by the police, frailly blocked his way. Christ, he thought, they're coming back for more measurements.

J.B. went into the children's bathroom. He looked at himself in the mirror for the first time in eight or nine hours. He was less surprised by the gray dirt that seemed to be pasted to his skin than he was by the dried blood creased across his forehead. He had forgotten about that injury, but wondered why all the people who had looked at him all night had failed to comment about it.

J.B. contemplated the prospects of a comfortable bath or shower in the children's bathroom, and amid the open toothpaste tubes, rubber toys in the tub, and Walt Disney decals on the wall, had just about decided that the prospects were not good when the telephone rang.

Limping back to the kitchen, he picked up the receiver. It was just after 6:00 a.m. and not the time for normal calls, unless it was some fool from the head office.

It was some fool from the head office. Apparently the murder at the American Club had made the international wire services, but the question of exactly who had been murdered was not clear. The report had indicated that it was "the head of the club."

"It wasn't you who was murdered, then?" queried the voice.

"No it wasn't," confirmed J.B.

"Good," said the voice, "because the divisional vice president will be arriving in Tokyo the day after tomorrow."

"No problem," said J.B., gaining slightly more insight into poor Gordy Sparks' frame of mind during the last few months.

J.B. began slicing the sausage in order to fry it along with the eggs when the idea struck him. He had clean exercise clothes in his locker at the club, and the prospects of a luxurious shower accompanied by perhaps a short session in the sauna would be just the thing to soak and bake the grime from his body. At this hour of the morning, the trip to the club would take just a few minutes. He turned off the burner under the frying pan, licked his fingers, but left the sausage and eggs on the counter. Breakfast could wait.

Climbing into Bumpy's little Honda was something of a chore. The sauna would certainly relieve the stiffness, and the relaxed sleepiness it was sure to produce would allow him to pass enough hours in an unconscious state so that the pain of fresh injuries would become the dull ache of old wounds.

It was somewhat macabre to contemplate what must have gone on in Butch's mind to prompt him to violently attack the Culhane family. On one hand, of course, there was the fact that Butch's wife had revealed to Bumpy the awful secret her husband had carried around with him all those years. A perverted sort of logic dictated that J.B.'s death would seal that

information away from public consumption and subsequent speculation about possible motives for
Pete's murder.

But logic probably had nothing to do with Butch's
behavior during the last seventy-two hours. Clearly
the Culhanes represented a stable family life that
Butch never had as a youngster. There was perhaps
an underlying factor that in some murky psychological way transformed J.B. into a father figure—at
least around the club—that Butch felt had to be
destroyed also. However one looked at it, normal
logic did not apply.

The club parking lot was nearly empty—the only
other cars on the premises belonged to the early-
morning squash fanatics. J.B. parked the Honda as
close as he could to the entrance of the recreation
building and dragged himself through the front door
and over to the reception desk. The attendant, looking both sunburned from an unanticipated Sunday
holiday and surprised because of the president's visit
so early in the morning, handed J.B. two thick towels.

One squash player in the locker room, late for his
game, asked J.B. as he was leaving for the courts if
any progress was being made in solving the general
manager's murder. J.B. could not bring himself to
say more than "not yet." "Shocking," was the man's
comment as he bounded from the room, all youth and
innocence.

J.B. punched the ON button activating the sauna
heating system as he headed for the shower room. It

occurred to him that as long as he was still president of the club, he would issue a directive to the squash players to the effect that tennis shoes should not be stored on the tops of lockers—the odor of sweat-soaked canvas and rubber was becoming overpowering in a room that should smell of talc and deodorant. The shoes should be taken home, or kept in car trunks, where rotting fabric would not be so publicly offensive.

The session in the love hotel with Midori flashed into J.B.'s consciousness as he stood under the stream of hot water in the shower. He had been exhausted then, but it was nothing like the feeling he was experiencing now. It's funny, J.B. reflected, Midori thought Pete was *his* boss. J.B. bent forward and let the driving warmth beat down on his injured back. Would Midori, he wondered, and all the other club employees, be "all ga-ga" over recent developments?

One question still remained, however, and that had to do with the whereabouts of Pete's headless body. It was inconceivable that Kawamura's minions, crawling throughout the length, breadth, and depth of the main building, inside and outside, had not come up with the remains of the central character in the whole drama. There were various locker rooms, the laundry, bakery shop, employee dormitories, the butchery area, pantry, hidden recesses in the kitchen, and all the mechanical support rooms to search, but everyone had come up empty-handed. It was as if the final insult to the man would be the extraordinary disappearance of all the structure beneath his neck. "Vanished into thin air," would be an apt but not very agreeable epithet for a club manager with a long and relatively distinguished career.

J.B. shut off the shower and padded across the synthetic carpet to the spacious, L-shaped sauna. He felt looser now than he had been before the heat and steam warmed his bones. In fact he now felt very hungry, and the prospect of the chef's sausage, eggs, toast, and coffee waiting at home elevated his spirits. J.B. made a mental note to try and convince the chef to make his sausage a regular part of the club menu. After all, J.B. reasoned, he was *still* the club president.

The blast of dry heat from the sauna as J.B. entered reminded him that he was still wearing his contact lenses. Soft lenses tended to stiffen in dry air, and J.B. glimpsed the reclining benches in brief flashes between the rapid blinking of his eyes. Something must be done about the damn tennis shoes in the locker room, he thought as he spread one of his towels on the lowest bench. The smell was disgusting.

It may have been two minutes, or it could have been as long as five minutes before the realization struck. J.B. had been leaning back with his eyes closed and focusing all attention on the sensation of the baking heat.

It was the shifting weight and rustle of clothes that brought to his awareness the surprising fact that he was not alone in the sauna. J.B. leaned forward and peered around the corner. One lens popped out as he stared at his companion.

*   *   *   *

It took four squash players, returning from their games, to calm the naked pink man hopping around the locker room. He had been screaming something about being the president of the club, and this diverted everyone's attention for several minutes. One of the squash players finally did check the sauna; that seemed to be what the wildly incoherent man wanted.

Seated in apparent calm, hands folded in his lap, tuxedo jacket neatly buttoned, one leg crossed over the other with the formally shod foot of the upper leg gently swinging as heat relaxed the rigor of muscle, was the other half of Pete Peterson.

— THE END —